KON

THE TRASSATO CRIME FAMILY, Book #2

BY LISA CARDIFF

KON

Limitless Publishing, LLC
Kailua, HI 96734
www.limitlesspublishing.com

Formatting: Limitless Publishing

ISBN-13: 978-1-68058-856-9
ISBN-10: 1-68058-856-7

CHAPTER ONE

Konstantin

"I need a fiancée like I need a fucking bullet in my head." I slammed the shot glass onto the burled walnut countertop.

A toxic combination of loud music and vodka swam through my veins like a drug. Rather than mellowing me out, it only made me angrier. God knew, I should drag my pathetic ass home before I did something to piss off my dad even more, yet I couldn't bring myself to move. So many things were wrong with my life I didn't know where to start. So I engaged in my favorite pastime as of late—drinking.

No matter how much I drank tonight, I couldn't forget my sister was getting married right now, and she didn't invite a single family member. Not me, not Mom, not Dad. Not even an estranged aunt or uncle.

I couldn't blame her. We'd toyed with her life behind the scenes for years. I threatened every boy in our high school that dared to look in her direction. Once she moved to New York, things weren't as simple. Her career took off, and we both had our own shit to deal with. Somehow she'd ended up engaged to a cheating, mealy-mouthed loser.

Granted, we could have handled things differently. I didn't have to set him up to fail. He would have managed that all on his own. I merely sped up the process, and I didn't regret it for a second. Better I sacrificed our relationship than have Evie waste the rest of her life on her piece of shit ex. Regardless of the fact that I made peace with my actions, I still missed my sister. While we hadn't spent much time together over the past few years, she'd always been in my thoughts.

I loved her. She'd been the one person I could always count on, and most importantly, she never had a hidden agenda when we spent time together. I couldn't say that about anyone else in my life. They had all disappointed me one way or another.

"We've already had this discussion. I'm done talking about it. Take the Trassato chick out a few times. Get to know her." Anatolyi shrugged. "If it works out, great. If not, tell your dad to go fuck himself. You know he won't make you marry her. I'd be hard pressed to find anyone who despises the concept as much as your dad. He'll come around."

"Then you don't know my dad very well. He's set on this dumb ass plan, and nothing's going to change his mind." I lifted my shot glass and pinned the bartender with a glare. I should have asked for the bottle when I walked in an hour ago so I didn't waste his time or mine. "Making money is the Holy Grail to my dad, and he's got it in his head that if I marry Carmela Trassato it'll give us more power and influence."

"Fine. Roll over like a dog and do what your daddy wants. You're too big of a pussy to challenge him, so you let him win every damn time." Anatolyi swiped a hand down the side of his face, bringing attention to the scar that stretched from his temple to his eyebrow. It made him look scary as fuck, but for some reason chicks dug it.

I pulled an envelope from my back pocket and slapped it on the counter. "Shut the hell up. I should kick your ass."

"Yeah, except you won't because without me, you'd be in the gutter somewhere licking your wounds." He twirled his drink. "I've saved your ass more times than I can count in past few months."

"Yeah, whatever, man." The bartender refilled my glass, and I chugged the clear liquid the minute he turned his back. "I haven't been that bad," I grumbled, my denial lacking conviction. Over the last few months, I started more bar fights than I could count, fucked more chicks than I could remember, and only my money and connections had kept me under the radar.

He threw his hands up. "You're fucking self-destructing."

"That shit's behind me now." I slid the envelope toward him. "I need a favor. I need you to find Carmela Trassato and—"

His eyebrows shot up, and he scraped his hands through his sandy blond hair. "I love you, man, but

I gotta be real honest with you. I'm not trading places with you if that's what you're thinking. I've seen some pictures of her, and she's not half bad, but I'm way too young to have a ball and chain. Not to mention, you foisted your ex off on me all the time." He shivered. "I don't want to be the third wheel in a relationship again, stuck taking care of your woman while you're off doin' business."

"Nah. That's not gonna happen." I pointed to the envelope. "Just deliver this to her. I can take care of the rest."

"Uh huh, and where will I find her? Because there's no way I'm going to knock on the Trassatos' door. I don't give a shit if her old man is dead. I'm not going there."

"You're going to my sister's wedding."

"Her wedding?"

"Yeah." I cracked my neck one way, then the other. "It's at some old mansion outside of the city. I'll text you the address."

"No way." He wagged his head, his dark eyes wide and his lips pressed into a thin line. "They'll have security everywhere."

"They do, but no one will be at the back door between eight and nine."

His eyebrows lifted. "How do you know that?"

I kept my gaze steady and my voice firm. "I'm that good."

"Fine. I'll do it, but you owe me…again." He glanced at his phone, then scooped it up and stuffed it into the pocket of his too-tight black jeans. He looked like a stupid hipster with his fitted shirt, tapered jeans, and straggly beard. "If I end up dead

4

I'll haunt your ass until the day you die."

"I wouldn't expect anything else." I snagged my black hoodie from the back of my chair. "Wear this so no one gets a good look at you."

CHAPTER TWO

Carmela

It should've been Rocco and me.

I loved my brother, and Evie had been my best friend for over two years. Despite them being my two favorite people in the world, I never could have imagined they'd wind up together. Not even in my wildest drug-induced dreams.

As far as I could tell, they had absolutely nothing in common. Evie was a small town girl with big city dreams, and Gian was up to his eyeballs in the business of loan sharking, killing, bribing, and whatever else my family did. I didn't know the details, and I was perfectly okay with that. Truthfully, I preferred it. I saw a glimpse of my family's depravity when the DiTonnos gunned downed Rocco, and that was more than enough to satisfy my morbid curiosity.

The music faded, and Gian dipped Evie, her strawberry blonde waves nearly sweeping the temporary dance floor, marking the end of their first dance. The all too familiar emptiness bubbled up my throat, and I didn't know if I'd choke or cry.

I should be happy for Evie and Gian. Just looking at the way they glowed and the perma-blush on Evie's cheeks would make any normal sister/maid of honor explode with happiness, except I wasn't normal. I felt sadder than I had since burying my fiancé, and I hated myself for feeling that way. I'd sacrificed any possibility of a happily ever after to ensure Gian and Evie could be together, or at least I thought I did. I hadn't heard a word from Konstantin Trincher or his father in thirteen months.

Thirteen fucking months.

Seriously, what was the deal with that?

Part of me hoped they had released me from the barbaric arranged marriage with Konstantin, and they simply forgot to notify me. Another part of me hoped he'd hurry up and get this over with so I could stop living in purgatory. Hell seemed preferable. And the other small part of me, the part I would never acknowledge, took pride in the fact that I had successfully negotiated a deal with the notorious Trinchers. It marked the first time in years I'd exercised my free will instead of blindly accepting my family's marching orders.

Stifling a heavy sigh, I dragged my spoon through my now lukewarm bowl of Italian wedding soup until the limp spinach and tiny meatballs blurred together in a miasma of brown and green. I couldn't stomach more than one bite.

Since I moved home to fill the aching loneliness of my dad's and Rocco's deaths, my lack of appetite took on a life of its own. I had to tailor my size eight bridesmaid's dress because it hung on me. Since I turned fourteen, I'd been on the curvy side, and I still was, but at this rate, I'd look like Evie with her dancer's body minus all the muscles in a matter of months.

Nobody noticed. Not Gian, not Evie, and certainly not my mom. She was so caught up in her grief, I might as well have been invisible. We orbited around each other in the vast space of my childhood home like two strangers passing in the night. When she wasn't crying, she spent every free second obsessing over the details of Gian and Evie's wedding.

I had stopped trying to communicate with her over a month ago. She was emotionally unavailable, and nothing I did would change it. She needed to find peace on her own, and somehow I needed to find mine since I didn't feel much of anything lately.

Rocco's death broke me, but my dad's death, the one I pretended would never happen, sealed my fate. Every day that passed, I felt deader than before. People claimed time healed all wounds. The more I thought about it, the more I was convinced they were totally wrong. In my opinion, time *caused* more wounds. The damage started small, with tiny nicks in my heart. Then they grew and grew until I had a black hole in the center of my chest, sucking and pulling on me until I couldn't think.

"Carmela?"

"Huh?"

I turned to Nico DeAngelo, my date for the

wedding. Technically, this qualified as our third or fourth date. Maybe more. I'd lost count. Like so many other things in my life, I didn't care. So what? Nico had taken me out couple of times. We hadn't kissed, though, and it felt like going out with a friend more than anything else.

Two weeks before my dad died nearly three months ago, he demanded I give Nico a chance. I wanted to say no. I needed to say no, but I couldn't because there was no way I could have confessed I'd agreed to some sort of relationship with Konstantin Trincher. He was already on edge about Gian's relationship with Evie. While Alix Trincher kept his word and backed off, my dad didn't believe he'd go away without a fight.

"Do you want to dance?" One corner of his lips perked up like he was the keeper of a million naughty secrets. By almost anyone's standards, Nico qualified as handsome. He had icy blue bedroom eyes, long lashes that actually curled, pouty lips, and an angular chin with the cleft in the dead center. I'd seen the way other women ogled him. Heck, my cousin Ava practically drooled every time she looked at him. She resorted to draping herself over him during the cocktail hour like a cheap dress, and I couldn't summon a flicker of jealousy. Without uttering a single objection, I walked away. She could have him. It'd save me a lot of trouble.

"I'm not done eating," I lied.

He held out one hand, palm up. "Dance with me." It wasn't a question. It was a demand, which didn't surprise me. As long as I'd known him, he never politely requested anything. He took what he wanted, and apparently he'd got it in his head that he wanted me.

I slipped my hand into his and followed him to the dance floor, joining five or six other couples. Grinning down at me, he closed his arms around my waist. I stared at him, hoping to feel something.

A quiver of my stomach. A double thud of my heart. A flicker of lust. A flare of disgust.

Any*fucking*thing.

When the couples started swirling into motion around us, I gave up and hooked my arms around his neck. We danced to a song about loving a man like you were going to lose him. I'd already lost the only man I'd ever love so the whole song felt depressing rather than romantic.

"You look beautiful," Nico murmured next to my ear.

"You think so?"

His hands tightened around my waist. "I do."

"Really?" I tipped up my head, catching his eyes. "I kind of thought canary yellow wasn't my color." I wasn't lying. It brought out the yellow undertone of my skin and made me look jaundiced.

He spun me away from him, probably to avoid responding to my comment, and snapped me back into his waiting arms.

"You look beautiful in any color," his said, brushing his thumb along my cheek.

A wave of heat rolled up my face and with it a spark of hope. Maybe a relationship with Nico would work. With his position in the Trassato family, he could untangle the promise I'd made to

Konstantin and maybe, just maybe, I'd be content, if not happy.

Nico froze mid-step. A hush fell over the room.

"What's going on?"

"Goddammit. I told her to stay away." His hands dropped from my waist and his eyebrows flattened into a straight line, highlighting the rigid pinch of skin in the middle.

"Who?" I glanced over my shoulder. A woman in a black shift dress with a young boy on her hip hovered near the entrance to the room. I squinted, trying to bring her into focus. "Wait. Isn't that your sister?"

I hadn't seen Nico's sister in years. She'd been banished from our life after she ended up pregnant three years ago. Apparently, she'd been dating some guy on and off again, and he split for good when he found out about her pregnancy, or least that was the rumor circulating about her.

I didn't understand why anyone considered it a big deal. She was twenty-four not sixteen, and there were plenty of successful single mothers in the world. Although it wasn't the kiss of death anymore, the *family* didn't see it that way. She disappeared from our circle of acquaintances and no one had seen her since. Until tonight.

Nico cut across the dance floor, his hands buried deep in the pockets of his black suit pants. Without thinking twice, I trailed behind him, wanting to defuse the situation. Nico normally kept a tight leash on his emotions, but from the stiff set of his shoulders, I feared he planned to draw blood. "Gemma," Nico growled. "What are you doing here?"

She shifted the little boy to her other hip. "I lost the keys to my apartment. I've called and texted you a hundred times, and you haven't responded. I didn't have any choice. It's not like I can sit at Lanelle's house all night with Marco Rocky. It's already past his bedtime, and you're the only one with a spare key."

"Rocky? His middle name is Rocky?" I blurted out, ignoring the way saying my dead fiancé's childhood nickname knifed through my chest. Seeing that he hated the nickname, only Rocco's mom and I used it. He thought it sounded childish, and had stopped acknowledging it by the time he turned twelve. Most people called him Rocco or Little Rock because he was named after his dad.

Her dark eyes cut to me, and her mouth contorted into what could only be called a snarl. "Nico, what are you doing with *her*?"

Nico patted her shoulder. "Come on, Gemma. This isn't the time or the place. I'll walk you out."

"Not until you tell me what's going on with Carmela Trassato." She spat my name like a dirty word.

"She's my date. Now, c'mon. Let's take this outside. Nothing good is gonna happen by staying here." His hand circled her upper arm, and he pulled her toward the exit.

"Your date?" She snatched her arm away. "Are you serious? Please tell me you're not serious. You wouldn't date her after everything, right?"

Clueless what I did to piss her off, my attention ping-ponged between Nico and his sister. I'd only met her a handful of times, and she was more Ava's friend than mine. They hung around a fast crowd, whereas my parents practically kept me under lock and key until I graduated from high school.

"What did I do?"

"You and your family did plenty." She lifted her finger, aiming it at me like a loaded gun, and I backpedaled a few steps.

"That's enough," Nico barked. "Carmela doesn't have anything to do with this. You made your bed, and if you want to see another dollar from me, you'll shut the fuck up and march your ass outta here right now."

She blinked away a few tears. "So that's it? You're choosing her over me too?"

The muscle in the lower half of his jaw ticking, Nico pulled a keychain from his pocket. "Grow up, Gemma. Not everything revolves around you."

Gemma's shoulders sagged, and she held out her open hand. "Fine. Whatever you say. Just give me the key, and I'll leave."

"Take my car." He dropped the keys into her palm. "I'll stop by later and we can talk."

She unthreaded a key and tossed the keychain at Nico's chest. It bounced off and clattered to the floor. "Lanelle's waiting outside. I don't need you or your stupid car. *Facia bruta*."

She spun on her heel and stomped away. What a drama queen.

"Sorry about that." Nico took my hand. "Are you okay?"

"What was that about?"

"Nothing. She's bitter about the way her life

turned out, and she doesn't have anyone to blame except herself. She made a lot of bad decisions over the past few years, and she refuses to accept responsibility and move on with her life."

"I'm going to the bathroom. I'll catch up with you in a few minutes."

"Don't worry about it. I need to talk to Dominick anyway. Come find me when you're ready to go."

He planted a kiss on the corner of my mouth. I drew his spicy scent into my lungs and hooked my hands around his neck. I kissed him back, barely a faint touch, lingering for a few seconds when a husky noise rumbled from his lips. He opened his mouth and moved his tongue against mine.

Deep. Possessive. Hungry.

It'd been too long since I kissed a man. Over three years to be exact. The last time I saw Rocco looped through my brain like a horror movie and I staggered back, ending the kiss. I blinked twice trying to bring everything into focus. I couldn't believe I had kissed Nico.

He squeezed my hand, a grin splashed across his face. "Go do what you need to do. I'll be waiting for you."

I nodded numbly and rushed out of the ballroom, ignoring the stares from the guests. I needed a few minutes alone and not only due to the weird confrontation with Nico's sister, but also because everyone's prying eyes were directed at me. I couldn't count the number of times people pumped me for information about when I planned to get married. I wished they'd shut up and mind their own business. So what? My twin brother beat me to the altar. I was twenty-eight, not thirty-eight. I had time.

"Carmela Trassato?" A man with a black hoodie and jeans stepped out of the shadows, and a chill darted down my spine.

"Yes?"

He shoved a white envelope against my stomach. "This is for you."

I frowned, tearing it out of his hand. "Who are you?"

"No one important." He turned, heading toward to exit.

I sat on a cobalt blue bench near the bathroom and ripped open the envelope, my hands shaking and dread suffocating me.

C.,

Meet me at Mercantile Restaurant at 6 tomorrow. We need to talk about the future.

-K.

"Fuck my life." I crumpled the note into a ball and tossed it into the trash.

CHAPTER THREE

Konstantin

More than fifteen minutes late, I scanned the restaurant for Carmela. As hard as I tried, I couldn't get my shit together today, mentally or physically. I drank too damn much last night, and my head throbbed like a motherfucker late into the afternoon. Then there was my visceral reaction to the thought of seeing Carmela, which only played into my reservations about following through with this arrangement.

I thoroughly enjoyed pretending Carmela didn't exist for the last year. That this whole mess would disappear if I ignored it. That she'd find someone else and my father would open his eyes and finally see the stupidity in this course of action.

Sadly, Evie's marriage to Gian thrust the bargain into the forefront of my dad's mind, renewing his interest in furthering our connection to the Trassatos. Now I didn't have any choice except to open communications with Carmela and hope this whole scheme didn't end with an engagement, or worse, marriage.

Granted, I had enough leverage to call my dad's bluff and refuse to follow through with this. Two things stopped me from doing exactly that. First, it would cause an irreparable divide between my dad and me, and he was the only family member still in my life. My mom called me maybe two times in the last year, my birthday and Christmas. She started dating some guy in my hometown, and she wanted to put some space between her past and present, which in her mind included me.

Secondly, my dad was unpredictable. He could go after Evie, and while Evie and I weren't on speaking terms, I didn't want anything bad to happen to her. She was my sister, and after everything we put her through—the lies, the half-truths, and manipulations—I owed it to her to shield her from our dad's poisonous interference.

This left me with one option. I had to find a way to placate my dad without getting sucked into an unwanted committed relationship. My last relationship demonstrated that nothing good came of welcoming people into your life and your soul. At best, it ended in disappointment. At worst, it left you with permanent scars.

My gaze finally landed on Carmela, and a jolt of electricity rocketed through me.

Damnit.

This was why I'd avoided this woman for months. I wanted her on some primal level, which was fine. I lusted after a lot of women since I kicked Laney out of my life. Hell, I screwed plenty of them, but none of them stuck in my head like Carmela Trassato, and I hadn't even touched her.

You know that flash of a second when your eyes connect with someone's and it's like your souls know each other? Well, I'd swear on pain of death that was what happened the first time I saw Carmela. I dismissed those convoluted feelings and moved on until my dad demanded I accompany him to the Trassatos' house before Carmela's dad died.

For weeks afterward, I saw her face every damn time I closed my eyes. Even worse, I smelled her clean, citrusy scent everywhere. As cheesy as it sounded, it was like she had cast a spell on me.

When I thought I had managed to scrub her from my brain permanently, my dad made a deal with her to let Gian pursue Evie in exchange for Carmela condemning herself to a life with me. Then my fixation with her started all over again, albeit this time around no amount of alcohol, fights, women, or near death experiences had helped to scrub her existence from my mind.

"Carmela," I grunted, sliding into the chair across from her. "You look nice." I lied. She looked better than nice. She embodied every fantasy I had when I was still a naïve farm boy living the simple life in Nebraska, and not a nasty criminal with a lengthy list of sins.

Exotic amber eyes that reminded me of sunshine. Long dark hair with the right amount of wave. Skin the color of golden honey. Curves that made my hands twitch with the urge to grab a handful. Lips the color of the forbidden fruit in the Garden of Eden.

And like the forbidden fruit led to Adam and Eve's ruin, I knew Carmela Trassato would be mine if I let down my guard around her.

"Mr. Trincher." The measured burn of her stare scraped down my torso and back up again as she dragged her finger through the condensation on her water glass. She wasn't touching me, yet I felt the swipe of her soft hands all the same. "Sorry I can't say the same about you. You look like shit. Did you attempt to drown yourself in a fifth of vodka last night or is this a standard look for you?"

Leaning back, I folded my arms across my chest and offered her my trademarked grin. It started at one corner and leisurely spread to the other. "Is that any way to treat the love of your life and your future husband?"

She recoiled and her elbow caught the edge of the table. The cutlery rattled and the water glasses wobbled. She closed her eyes momentarily and hitched a breath. "Is that why you're here? Did you finally decide to go through with this?"

"Not exactly."

"What do you mean?"

She studied me, and beneath the layers of distrust I saw hope. I saw happiness. I saw excitement. My gut twisted with the need to be the prince charming for once in my godforsaken life. Unfortunately for her, circumstances had already cast me as the villain, and I didn't think that would change any time in the near future.

"Look, Carmela." I planted my hands on the edge of the table. "I don't want to marry you, I don't want to date you, and I definitely don't want to grow old with you."

The corner of her lips curled upward, and she beamed with gullibility and innocence. "So that's it? The deal is off. Both of us are free to do whatever we want?"

"If only that were the case."

Her brows caved together. We were so close that only the flickering candle and waves of heat separated our faces. "Then why am I here?"

The waitress approached the table, her hands on her hips and an overly bright smile on her face. She looked vaguely familiar. "Hey, Kon," she purred, her expression predatory. "Where have you been hiding yourself?"

Then it hit me, and I grimaced inwardly. This chick had sucked me off in the storage room the last time I came here for dinner with my dad a couple of months ago. From what I could remember, the night was a real shit show. I'd pounded back drink after drink while my dad ranted nonstop about the ways I had failed to meet his expectations, and how I never *would* meet his expectations. In other words, it was a typical night.

I pulled in more money than my dad and my influence in the Russian mafia was quickly eclipsing his, and yet he still wanted more, bleeding me dry every second I spent under his thumb. Instead of listening, I mercilessly flirted with the waitress, showing him without words he couldn't control me.

I whispered crude pickup lines every time she delivered something to the table. I brushed my fingertips up her bare legs and down her arm. And in retrospect, I acted like a complete dickhead.

When I got up to go to the bathroom, she redirected me to a nearby closet and proceeded to give me one of the most forgettable blowjobs of my life, but that didn't stop me from throwing it in my dad's face. He flipped his shit. I smiled at the memory of his face when I returned to the table.

"Here and there," I drawled, lifting the menu and for practical purposes dismissing her. I didn't need the ghosts of stupid decisions thrown in my face tonight. Not when I needed Carmela to trust me.

The waitress didn't get the hint. She inched closer and angled her body toward mine, her legs and plastic breasts sweeping against me. Her peppery, floral scent curled into my nose, and I ground my teeth together. She needed to back away before I flipped my shit.

"I haven't seen you around since we—"

"We're ready to order," I interrupted.

Carmela's curious stare fixed on the waitress whose name I couldn't recall even if someone pressed a gun to my head. "We are?" Carmela said. "Huh. I kind of wanted to hear what—I'm sorry I didn't catch your name…"

"Lindsey," the waitress supplied, rolling her shoulders back. Her breasts looked like they'd explode out of her white collared shirt with one strenuous breath.

"…Lindsey had to say about the last time you ran into her," Carmela finished.

"Lindsey," I said, drawing out her name, "doesn't have anything to say. She's here to do her job and take our order. We'll have the tasting menu with wine pairing."

"That's not happening," Carmela cut in. "It's seven courses. I don't have time for that."

Neither did I, but I in the interest of getting the waitress the hell away from me, I ordered the first item listed on the menu.

I turned to the waitress. "Why are you still here? I didn't ask you to pull up a chair and join us."

"Ugh. Whatever," she huffed, whirling around and stomping to the kitchen.

"Well, that was interesting," Carmela said. "Are you going to tell me what that was about?"

"There's nothing to tell."

There wasn't. Lindsey was one more woman in a lengthy line of mistakes since my ex shit all over my life, leaving my personal life in shambles. The only upside of my ex's departure was that I channeled my anger and resentment into making money, thinking I'd show my ex what she was missing.

Regrettably, flaunting my success came back to haunt me during Laney's first stint of sobriety and every one following. It never failed. She came after me like a stage five clinger, meddling in my life and trying to worm her way back into my home. I made the mistake of helping her out once, and I'd never repeat it. She stole everything of value in my place, and disappeared.

"Actually, you know what? I don't want to know what that was about. Just cut to the chase. What's going on here? I don't get it. You don't want anything to do with the deal I made with your dad, but you want to sit here for three hours, doing what? Staring at each other?"

"I said I didn't want anything to do with the arrangement, but that doesn't mean I won't go through the motions if I have to."

"Go through the motions?"

"We're going to date. You know, pretend we plan to fulfill the terms of the agreement until we find a way out of this."

"How will dating help anything?"

"It will get my dad off my back." I pinched the bridge of my nose and released a strained breath. My headache from drinking too much last night roared back to life with a vengeance. "Right now, he's pushing to announce the engagement as a way to force your family to the negotiating table. I don't want that, and I'd bet my life you don't either."

"He can't do that. My family would freak. It would be ugly. And I've gone on a few dates with someone else recently. It would look suspicious. They'd never buy it."

A surge of unexpected and unwanted jealousy rushed through my veins. "Dates with who?"

She licked her lips, then lifted her glass of ice water. I couldn't look away. Something about the way her full lips curled around the glass made my pulse rate skyrocket. Images of her on her knees with her lips parted, looking at me with those amber eyes through the fringe of her lashes flashed through my brain.

"I can do whatever I want with whomever I want. It's none of your business," she said, squashing the depraved spiral of my thoughts as effectively as throwing a cold glass of water in my face.

"Like hell, it isn't." I snatched her wrist. "Don't fuck with me. I didn't get where I am by being a pushover."

"No, I suspect you got where you are with a little nepotism and a whole lot of murder."

I released my grasp. "Don't push me. Trust me. You won't enjoy the consequences."

She cocked a brow. "Oh, yeah? Is that a threat, Mr. Trincher? Because if it is I'd like to remind you I'm not some powerless twit. I can rain Hell down on you with the snap of my fingers."

"Have it your way." I tossed my napkin on the table. "I'll tell my dad to go ahead and announce our engagement. I don't give a fuck."

"Ugh." She threw her hands up. "Fine. Don't be such an ass. I've gone on a few dates with Nico DeAngelo."

"Are you fucking kidding me?"

"What's wrong with Nico?"

I snorted. Of all the men she could be dating in this city or in her circle of acquaintances, she decided to explore something with Nico DeAngelo. He was a manipulative bastard. Every move he made was calculated to line his pockets. Dominick held the title godfather in the Trassato family, but Nico had his greedy fingers in everything, distorting the truth to his benefit. Dominick was dumb as fuck if he actually trusted him. He was doing thousands of dollars of business off the record, and Dominick either ignored it or was too senile to see it.

"So many things I don't know where to start."

"Why don't you give it a stab?"

"I'll let you figure out his flaws for yourself."

"Does that mean you won't interfere in our relationship?"

"So now you're in a relationship." The word tasted like poison on my tongue.

"Not really." Her shoulders dipped, and she unfolded her napkin, dropping it in her lap. "My dad wanted me to marry him. My uncle has given his official nod of approval. I've been dragging my feet, but if I can get out of this thing with you, it's probably a done deal. That's how things work in my family."

"Do you like him?"

"He's okay, not that it matters what I do or don't like."

She chewed on the corner of her lip, her gaze flitting around the restaurant. In that second, I saw straight through her tough exterior, and the misery in her eyes squeezed at that big organ in the center of my chest. Here was this completely stunning woman with her dark hair, glowing eyes, the perfect amount of curves, living a charmed life without many responsibilities or financial hardship, yet you'd think she had nothing and no one. Some previously undetected piece of me that gave a damn about people wanted to pull her into my arms and erase her pain. I squashed the thought as quickly as it surfaced. I didn't have time for sentimental emotions. They kicked my ass before, and they'd do it again if I didn't keep myself firmly in check.

"Well, that's a ringing endorsement if I've ever heard one."

Her nose scrunched up in exasperation. "Why do you care?"

"I don't." I scrubbed my hand down my face, trying to wipe away any lingering jealousy, attraction, or whatever else I felt for her. I needed to get my head on straight when it came to this woman. I couldn't let any ill-conceived feelings get in the way of doing what needed to be done. "In fact, this whole thing could work to our benefit."

"What do you mean?"

"Let me worry about the details."

Her eyes veered to the side, and she folded her arms across her chest, calling attention to the soft rise and fall of her chest. "No. I won't blindly follow along with some scheme you're concocting in your head."

"Well, that's too fucking bad. You should've have thought about that before you agreed to my dad's plan."

"You're an asshole."

"So you've said. What's your point?"

She stared at me in silence for a few moments. It unnerved me sitting across from her after months of simultaneously cursing her existence and craving her. Soft music mixed with the low rumble of conversation floated through the room. Her scent reminded me of the lemon trees in my mom's greenhouse when they blossomed.

"You know what? I don't care what you have in mind if it ends with you out of my life."

"It might if we play our cards right."

She swallowed, but it looked more like she had eaten something rotten. "When do we start?"

"You'll meet me at an event in two days. I'll text you the details."

"What kind of event?"

"A little something with business associates. I'll introduce you to some people. We'll plant the seed that we're more than friends. If things go to plan, we'll be able to unwind this whole thing and move on to bigger and better things."

"Perfect. I can't wait. Now cancel the tasting menu. I'm leaving." She stood. "Or better yet, why don't you enjoy it with Lindsey? It sounds like she's dying for another round with you."

CHAPTER FOUR

Carmela

It took way too long for me to get ready for my date with Konstantin Trincher. Other than his curt text instructing me to dress up and meet him at a bar on a sketchy block under a bridge at nine sharp, I didn't have a clue what he had planned.

At eight-thirty, I settled on a red dress with a diagonal cutout around one side of my waist and strappy gold heels. After playing with a bunch of different hairstyles, I parted my hair down the middle and called it a day, reminding myself I didn't care what that man thought of me.

With one last look at the clothes piled on my bed and jewelry scattered across the top of my dresser, I pulled out my phone, tapped on the closest car available, and jogged down the stairs.

"Carmela," my mom called out the minute my hand curled around the door handle.

"Yes?" I glanced over my shoulder.

"Where are you off to?"

Fighting the urge to groan, I turned to face her. My dad's personal belongings were still sprinkled around the house like he was on an extended vacation and he'd be back any day. His black tasseled loafers sat next to the front door. His favorite overcoat hung on a hook near the entrance to the library. His book was on the end table, the bookmark still tucked inside. I needed to get out of this place. It was like someone had waved a magic wand, freezing everything in a permanent cycle of grief, myself included. If I stayed here, I'd never move forward.

"I'm meeting a friend for dinner."

She looked at me, taking in my appearance. "Nico?"

"No. A friend from design school."

Her eyes narrowed, and I cursed my bad luck. For months, my mom couldn't be bothered with me, and now when I truly needed her to be indifferent, she'd decided to take an interest in me. I should have exited through the garage instead of the front door.

"Does your friend have a name?"

"Mom." I spread my arms wide, my red clutch in one hand and my phone in the other. The gold bangles on my arm jingled. "What's with all the questions?"

She tucked a glossy covered magazine under her arm. "I know I've been emotionally unavailable since your father died. Honestly, I didn't want to face the reality of spending the rest of my life alone, so I focused all my energy on Gian and Evangeline's wedding. Now that it's over, I see that you've been hurting too. First Rocco, and now your dad. I'm sure it hasn't been easy for you. I want to be there for you and help you get your life back on track. You're too young to give up on happiness. Rocco wouldn't want that. Your dad didn't want that either. We talked about your future a lot in those weeks before he died, you know."

Pain coiled around my chest like a vise, the never-ending misery suffocating me. I didn't want to talk about this right now. I'd lost two of the most important men in my life in less than three years. While I still had Gian, our relationship had changed since Evie came into his life. I didn't begrudge his happiness. How could I? I loved him more than anyone. Yet, as luck would have it, his happiness had the perverse side effect of shining a spotlight on my hollowness.

"No, it hasn't been easy." I shifted my weight from one foot to the other. "But I'm working through it. You don't need to worry about me."

She smiled, although it didn't reach her eyes. It never made it as far as her eyes anymore. "How are things with Nico? You looked cozy at the wedding. Your dad would be so happy to see the two of you together. He respected Nico. He's a hard worker and loyal to a fault."

"I know. Dad said as much before he died, but I don't want to rush into anything. I signed up for some interior design classes this fall, and I want to focus on finishing my degree."

"Have you talked to Nico about this? I'm pretty sure he won't like the idea of you working outside the home. Rocco didn't either."

I couldn't listen to this. I was so sick of being controlled by the men in my life. Rocco and my father made it very clear they didn't want me to work. After everything that happened, I thought I had earned the right to make decisions for myself. I wasn't a dumb twenty-year-old anymore. I knew what I wanted, and it wasn't sitting home while my husband went out and did God knew what. If I couldn't have love, I needed a career so at least some portion of my life had meaning.

"Mom, Nico and I aren't serious. We're taking things slowly, and if the last couple of years have taught me anything, it's that I can't rely on him or any other man to support me. I need to do my own thing. Be my own person. I want to have a life outside of the man I marry."

"Carmela, that sounds nice and all, but you're old enough to understand the way things work in this family. Nico plans to marry you. He and your father worked out the details months before he died. Nico agreed to give you time to get to know him and get accustomed to the idea. It's going to happen, though, and you need to be prepared."

My mouth hinged open, and my breath whooshed out of my lungs. "Are you serious?"

"Of course." She sighed like she had a hundred pound weight on her shoulders. "Your dad wanted to see you settled and make sure you were taken care of. I want that too. There's nothing wrong with that."

My fingers twitched with anger. I needed to get out of here before I said something I'd regret. "Listen, Mom, I understand you want what's best

31

for me, but I won't marry Nico because that's what you guys think is best for me. I need to feel something for him."

I cringed inwardly at my choice of words. I didn't expect my feelings for Nico or any other man to rival my connection with Rocco. Having those feelings for another man would be a betrayal to Rocco, his memory, and the life we planned together since childhood. All the same, I needed to feel some level of affection and respect for the man I eventually married.

My mother grabbed my hand and squeezed it, a slight tremor in her hand. "You're too young to give up on love, and Nico cares about you. If you open your heart to him, you might find something like you had with Rocco, or at the very least something that fills the emptiness."

"You don't know that."

"I'm your mother. I can see these things. Don't be stubborn. Give Nico a chance."

"I have been, Mom. In case you missed it, I've gone out with him more than a few times. I took him with me to Gian's wedding. So stop pushing me. I won't let you or anyone else force me into a relationship with someone I don't care about."

"You don't feel anything for Nico?"

"I don't know." I pushed my hair away from my face, regretting I didn't put it into a ponytail. It had grown too long over the past six months, and it hung in my face more often than not. "I haven't decided either way."

"Have you dated anyone else since Rocco died?"

Kon's blue eyes flashed through my mind. I

should have told my mother about my agreement with the Trinchers months ago, except the right moment never came. Initially, I didn't want to add to her pain. She had enough on her plate without worrying about some dumb deal I made to help Gian and Evie. As more and more time passed, I had hoped it would all disappear and I'd never have to confess what I'd done out of desperation to help my brother, completely disregarding my own safety in the process.

"Not really. I mean, I went to dinner with someone recently. Nothing will come of it. He's not interested in anything serious."

"Does Nico know?"

The car service honked.

Thank God.

"That's my ride. I'll talk to you tomorrow."

She pressed a gentle kiss to my forehead, and for the first time in months I felt like I had a mother again. "Okay. Have fun tonight. I love you."

"Love you too."

CHAPTER FIVE

Konstantin

"Rough night already?" Anatolyi squeezed my shoulder.

I flexed my hand around my drink, focusing on the entrance of the bar. Carmela was late, which wasn't a good thing. I needed to be downstairs to supervise the gambling festivities in the next ten minutes or my dad would get an earful from our VIPs, and as a rule, I liked to avoid confrontations with him. He was a malicious bastard when people didn't bend to his will.

Most dads yelled when they were ticked off. My dad had a tendency to pistol whip me or threaten to cut me out of his life. Although I must say, his relentless intimidation had gotten old, and I'd stopped taking him seriously approximately six months ago when it became painfully obvious he needed me as much as I needed him.

"Fuck off, Anatolyi." I shrugged out of his grasp. "Go make yourself useful somewhere, preferably far away from me."

He guffawed, pointing his beer bottle at me. "How cute. This woman already has you tied up in knots and you're not even fucking her." He scanned my face. "You're nervous she won't show."

"She'll show."

"If you say so."

He tapped his fingers to the beat of the music on the thigh of his grubby jeans. I'd never understand why my dad opened a Miami Beach themed bar in the armpit of Brooklyn. Latin percussion sounds pumped from speakers and the staff dressed the part with big tropical prints. On top of all that, they served fruity island cocktails decorated with slices of watermelon and pineapple.

The hipster crowd loved it. They thought they'd found a unique gem in the middle of Brooklyn, catering to their whims. In truth, the bar served as a front for the more profitable gambling activities in the bowels of this dump.

VIPs entered through the back door after reciting the secret password that changed nightly. Someone ushered them downstairs, and that's where the magic happened. Gambling. Drinking. Smoking. And a shitload of women dressed in next to nothing.

In fact, it looked like a seedy Las Vegas casino complete with blackjack tables, roulette wheels, poker tables, and an area dedicated to betting on everything from professional sports to the next president of the United States.

"Here she comes now." Anatolyi whistled, his head moving unhurriedly from side to side. "You better keep an eye on her tonight. The VIPs will think she's on the menu."

My head popped up, and everyone disappeared except Carmela. The red number she wore hugged every curve, and that little flash of skin on her right side made me want to peel off her clothes and lick every golden inch of her body. Her wavy brown hair brushed her breasts with every step. To top it off, her lips were painted ruby red, which made my mouth water and blood rush to my cock.

"Shit," I mumbled under my breath.

"Shit is right," he responded a grin spreading across his face. "I think I've changed my mind about trading places with you. She'd make a damn good ball and chain."

I elbowed him in the gut and he grunted. "Go away. I don't want to look at your ugly mug anymore tonight."

He took a few steps back with his hands up, his smile bigger than seconds before. "Fine, I'm outta here. You know where to find me if you need me."

"Hi, Konstantin," Carmela said. She tucked a strand of her hair behind her ear as she surveyed the room. "I've never been here before. It's an interesting place, that's for sure."

"You like it?"

"Um…" She angled her head and rolled her lips into her mouth. "Not so much."

I splayed my hand over my chest. "No? I'm devastated. I was trying to impress you. Oh, and call me Kon. I don't like people using my full name. It's too formal."

"So *Kon…*" She waved her hand toward the dance floor where a few couples twirled and shimmied to the music. "Are you planning to show me your moves?"

"No." I downed the rest of my drink, savoring the burn. "We're going downstairs, unless you want a drink first."

She eyed the fruity cocktail adorned with fuchsia and turquoise umbrellas. "No, I'm good."

I slotted my fingers through hers. They were cold to the touch and slightly shaky. "Then let's get going."

"Ah, excuse me." I tightened my hand when she tried to break my hold. "What are you doing?"

"We're dating. This is what couples do when they date."

"We are?"

I tugged her against my side. "It's part of the plan. Go with it," I whispered against the crook of her neck, enjoying the feel of her soft skin against my lips and the ever-present hint of lemon in her hair.

She shuddered, then tipped up her chin and started walking again. "I already know I'm going to regret this."

"Nah, this is gonna to be fun."

My dad would shit when he realized I brought Carmela here. Gian had stolen a handful of our high rollers last year, which pissed him the fuck off. Unfortunately for him, he'd have to bite his tongue when it came to Carmela, and let the enemy roam freely in his kingdom because I was following his orders like a good little soldier.

He wouldn't shut up about moving forward with my engagement with Carmela, and I was finally giving him what he wanted. I invited her into our den of iniquity. She could see firsthand what being tied to the Russian mafia meant. That alone might make her run screaming into the night. Although she had a brother and father elbow deep in the dealings of the Trassato crime family, there was no way either of them let her get anywhere near the action. They liked to keep their women in a bubble and blow sunshine up their asses until they ended up in prison or dead.

I nodded to the bouncer standing in front of the door to the basement, and he held up his hand.

"She on the list?"

Glaring, I released Carmela's hand. "She's with me." I cracked my knuckles on one hand then the other.

"You know how Mr. Trincher is about sticking to the list. I'd hate to piss anyone off."

I closed the distance, coming nose to nose with this punk. "Yeah, and I don't give a shit. She's with me, and that's all that matters. Do I need to explain how things work around here? I have final say on the guests now, not my father."

Over the last year, I'd taken over the gambling and black market export side of the business while my dad concentrated on the seedier stuff: drugs, particularly heroin, and human trafficking. After the shit that had gone down with Laney, I didn't want anything to do with pushing drugs.

My dad wouldn't give that up if he were on his deathbed. He loved playing God, warping futures, and ruining lives, and drug importing and pushing was where it all started for him. They were his roots. The other stuff—the more sophisticated crime and scams—came later. They were my brainchild. Where my dad was about muscle and pushing vices, I was about numbers and the chess game of outsmarting the system, finding loopholes, and exploiting weaknesses.

Groaning, he punched a code into the pad on the door and opened it. "Have a good night."

"We will."

CHAPTER SIX

Carmela

I paused at the foot of the stairs, my eyes adjusting to the dim lighting and the plumes of smoke. The sickly sweet stench of cigars burned my lungs, the steady drum of music shook the floors beneath my feet, and the roar of conversation and laughter bombarded my ears.

Women clad in boy shorts with glittery star pasties on their breasts glided around the room carrying trays filled with drinks held high over their heads. But instead of the attention being focused on those women, it was on me. Greedy eyes crawled over me like I had unknowingly volunteered to be their next snack, and the hair on the back of my neck lifted.

"What's this place?" I squeezed Kon's upper arm, my fingernails digging into his rope-like muscles, so hard and firm.

My mind pleaded with me to take off. I wasn't naïve. While my family had their hands in illegal gambling rackets and all sorts of other unsavory crap, I didn't want to see it firsthand, and I definitely didn't want to waste my Friday experiencing it.

His arm locked around my torso, his fingers landing on the bare skin near my waist. I clenched my teeth, willing my reaction to his touch away, yet for some godforsaken reason, goose bumps pebbled my skin.

"A place for the guys to let off steam after a long day of work."

"I want to leave." I shifted closer to him, plastering my front to his side. I'd crawl inside him if he'd let me. That's how bad I didn't want to be here.

"You'll be fine. Do you like blackjack?" he answered, his lips a hairsbreadth from my temple. A shockwave arrowed straight to my belly.

"Yeah, sure."

"Perfect."

He tugged me toward a half circle table with a dealer on one side and six men clad in everything from jeans and leather jackets to starched suits on the other. One empty chair sat directly in the middle of them.

Lucky me.

He pulled out the chair and gestured for me to sit. "Gentlemen, this is Carmela. Treat her well or you'll answer to me."

A chorus of greetings echoed in my ears, but I couldn't look away from Kon. I yanked on his arm, pulling him closer to me, which only served to make me entirely too distracted by his lips and too blue eyes. "Are you leaving me here?"

"For about a half an hour or so. I need to do the rounds, then I'll come and get you, and we'll go out to dinner."

My fingernails dug into the threads of his black collared shirt. "No. I don't want to play. I'm not a big fan of wasting my money." While I loved a good card game, I couldn't afford to lose any money. I was saving every dollar from my side business to move out of my mom's house again. I had a taste of independence before my dad died with my own life and apartment in the city. I needed that again or I'd lose my mind.

"No problem." He pulled a money clip from his pocket and plopped a wad of hundreds on the table in front of me. For a beat, I stared, unmoving. His tattooed hand captivated me, so large, and strong. I couldn't look away from the tiny stars, crosses, and swirling designs.

I opened my mouth to object, except I didn't have the chance. His head dipped closer, and his lips were on mine. I stopped breathing for a fraction of a second, and I fully intended to break contact, only I didn't. The increasingly familiar pull between us dragged me under like quicksand.

One graze, and I startled, electricity crackling through my nerve endings. A quick nip of his teeth, and he stole my breath. Seconds. Minutes. Hours. I didn't know how much time passed with his mouth lingering against mine, his exhalations becoming my inhalations. My head buzzed and my lips tingled, but worst of all, he tasted good—full and smoky, like whiskey and sin, except a thousand times more lethal. One of my hands cupped the side of his face, silently willing him not to stop. His stubble felt like sandpaper beneath my fingers.

After months, maybe years, of feeling nothing, I felt a spark of something and my heart softened a little toward him.

Fuck.

"Good luck, *solnyshka,*" he whispered as he broke away, his voice rough and low. It vibrated through me from the top of my head all the way to the soles of my heel-clad feet, rippling into the floor, and I felt unsteady for a beat like my entire world had shifted without my permission.

"Are you ready to play?" the dealer asked, his translucent blue eyes frosty.

"Yes." I swallowed back my confusion, mentally chalking up the whole moment to being an emotionally starved psycho who fabricated feelings in my head, kind of like the emotional equivalent of a mirage in the desert.

I peeled five hundreds from the pile and slid them across the table. With magic-like hands, the dealer replaced them with a stack of chips. Not knowing the table betting limit or minimum, I glanced at the man next to me and matched his bet.

Cards swooshed from the dealer's hand, brightening the emerald green table with splashes of red. Within minutes, I got lost in the strategy of the game, deciding whether to hit, stay, split or surrender.

"Hey," the man adjacent to me said.

"Hi." I peeked at him from the corner of my eye, but otherwise kept my attention fixed directly in front of me. He looked like a meathead with a dark unibrow and rubbery lips.

In less than thirty minutes, I had burned through half of my money. I hoped Kon didn't expect me to pay him back.

"So you and Konstantin Trincher, huh?" My hand froze mid-swish of my finger as I requested another card from the dealer. He leaned closer to me, and I nearly gagged on the tangy scent of his cologne.

"We're friendly." I shifted closer to the man on the opposite side of me, my foot bouncing up and down under the table. "That's it."

"You look familiar."

I ignored him and snuck a quick look at my new card instead.

Busted.

I signaled to the dealer that I was out.

"Yeah. I get that a lot." I didn't, but I had no intention of prolonging the conversation with this man.

He squeezed my upper thigh under the table, and I nearly jumped out of my seat. "I find that hard to believe. You don't see eyes like yours every day."

I scoured the room, desperately looking for Kon. "Well, thanks. I guess." I pushed my chips across the table. "Cash me out."

He stretched out his arm along the back of my chair and tugged on a strand of my hair. "Where are you running off to? This was just starting to get good."

I stared at the dealer, silently willing him to move faster. When he placed a stack of money in front of me, I peeled off a twenty and scooped the rest into my purse without counting it.

"It was nice meeting you," I called out as I half-ran, half-walked away from the table.

After spending a couple of minutes searching for Kon, I gave up and retreated to the bathroom where I retouched my lipstick and scrolled through my recent emails and texts.

Other than a quick text from Nico asking if I wanted to go out to dinner tomorrow night and piles of spam, I didn't see anything of importance. I didn't expect otherwise. Evie and Gian were on their honeymoon, my mom probably went to sleep right after I left, and other than Ava and Nico, nobody contacted me these days.

At twenty-eight, my family considered me an old maid, and for the most part, they had written me off as a lost cause. That probably explained their shared enthusiasm for Nico's interest in me even though most people in our circle of friends and family had misgivings about him. His reputation wasn't pretty. Over the years, I'd heard more than a few rumors about his brutality. Granted, I'd never seen anything firsthand, and he behaved like a gentleman every time I'd seen him.

I stuffed my phone back in my purse and pushed open the door. Kon probably noticed I was missing by now, and I didn't enjoy the thought of a confrontation with him. Whereas Nico appeared cold and calculating, Kon gave me the impression that his temper ran hot and quick.

"I knew I recognized you."

I halted mid-stride, my hand still pressed against

the inside of the door. The man from the card game stood at the end of the hall, his hands deep in his pockets and his eyebrows raised expectantly.

"I think you're confusing me with someone else."

"No." He halved the spaced between us. My nerves frazzled, I backpedaled, loosening the pressure on the door. It swung inward in a blur of dark brown, clipping my toes on the way and making me stumble backward. Before it fully shut, he smacked the palm of his hand against the slab of wood, forcing it open.

"You're Carmela Trassato, Rocco's fiancée. Well, not anymore. He's dead so I guess that would make you his not quite widow."

"Um, yeah." I edged back until I hit the wall. "Did you know Rocco?"

He rocked onto his heels, and his lips curled over his teeth in what I think he meant to be a smile, but it looked more like a snarl. "You could say that."

I peeked over his shoulder, looking for Kon or anyone. The hall to the bathroom was empty, which only served to increase my growing unease. I didn't like anything about this guy from his empty eyes to his mocking lips. He gave me the creeps.

"Oh really? What's your name?"

"Renzo DiTonno."

My heart stalled, then restarted, beating like it fully intended to leap out of my chest and splatter on the floor. A whole-body tremor rocketed through me. While nobody had shared the details of who killed Rocco with me, I did know the DiTonnos had a hand in his murder, which resulted in a yearlong war between our families. Dominick had negotiated a truce, but there could still be animosity on both sides, and I didn't want to step into a minefield unknowingly. Situations like this explained why my family kept such a rigid leash on me.

I swallowed back the nausea climbing up my throat. "That name doesn't sound familiar. If you'll excuse me, I have to find Kon. We have dinner reservations, and he wouldn't appreciate finding me huddled in the bathroom with another man. He's possessive like that."

It was a lie. I didn't have any evidence suggesting Kon gave a shit what I did. He didn't know that, though. I swerved around his body, darting in the direction of the door. Barely two strides later, his hand clamped around my upper arm, halting my retreat.

"And here I thought you claimed you two were only friends. Tsk. Tsk. What would your family think of you slumming it with Russian scum? Better yet, what would Nico DeAngelo think? I heard you two have been *friendly* lately. I heard you're the next golden couple in the Trassato family, destined to inherit everything."

"Get your hands off of me!" I jerked my arm up, trying to break his hold. It didn't work. He strengthened his grip, his fingertips digging into my arm with enough force to leave a bruise.

He wrenched my arm behind me and shoved my hips into the sink. He bent forward, his lips brushing the shell of my ear. I could smell whiskey and cigarettes on his breath, and I barely checked the instinct to gag. "Listen here, Dominick and Nico

47

may think this shit is over between our families, but that's far from the truth. Someone killed my brother and I won't stop until that motherfucker is in the ground. Do you hear me?"

I squeezed my eyes shut and turned my head to the side. "I don't know what you're talking about. Really. I promise."

"You Trassatos are all cut from the same cloth. You're a bunch of backstabbing pieces of shit."

The bathroom door flung open, hitting the wall with a loud *thud.* "What the fuck is going on here?" Kon roared, the muscle in his jaw twitching and his blue eyes icy. He looked intimidating as hell with his tattooed hands, scarred knuckles, and the small bend in his nose. All of it put together told the story of a man not afraid to fight and get his hands dirty, and right now I prayed he'd channel all that aggression to getting Renzo away from me.

CHAPTER SEVEN

Konstantin

Blood pulsed through me violently, mimicking the roar of a plane engine in my ears. My vision narrowed. Three steps and I had my hand curled around the collar of this asshole's shirt. I yanked him to the side, flinging him into the metal bathroom stalls.

"What the hell, man?" He held his hands up in surrender. "Miss Trassato and I were talking. That's it."

"Is that true, Carmela?"

"H-h-he…" A sob hiccupped from her mouth, and my rage multiplied, coating my vision in a haze of crimson. "He threatened me."

Although I was pissed when I walked in, it didn't compare to what I felt right now. I lunged at Renzo DiTonno, hammering him into the bathroom stall twice.

Bang. Rattle. Shake.

His fist snapped up, connecting with my jaw. My

49

head whipped to the side. Who the fuck did this guy think he was? He'd pay for this. Nobody came into my domain, my world, and manhandled my date or took a cheap shot at me. He was as good as dead.

The DiTonnos needed to keep their people in line or I would grind them into the dirt. My dad cut a deal with them when they were at war with the Trassatos, and we expanded our business with them from pushing drugs in their territory to bigger stuff.

In the process, I got a little cozy with some of the guys. We had similar business interests, and we all banked some serious cash scratching each other's backs. Now that the war with the Trassatos was over, I didn't know how long our arrangement would last. I didn't care either way. If they pulled back, I had other people waiting in line to do business with us.

I rammed the heel of my hand into the tip of his nose. The loud cracking sound bounced off the white tiled walls and blood spurted out of his nostrils. I grabbed my switchblade from my pocket, flipped it open, and pressed it against his neck, gawking with sick fascination when a drop of blood trickled onto the collar of his shirt.

"Either you're dumb as a stick or you have balls of steel coming into my bar and pulling this shit."

He grabbed my wrist, pushing the knife away from his throat. "The Trassatos are liars. Every single one of them. I don't care what Alesio wants. I won't share air with them. They killed my brother for no fucking reason."

"I don't give a shit what they did. They could've cut off your dick and mailed it to your mother. It doesn't matter to me. When you walk through *my* door, you play by *my* rules. You're here to gamble, not settle scores, especially with women. Got it?"

"You're gonna defend her? She's probably spying on you for that crazy bastard Nico. Everyone knows he plans to marry her. It's only a matter of time. She's toying with you."

"You really think I need dating advice from you?"

Hearing Nico's name pissed me the hell off. I pushed Renzo, and he dropped to his knees. I kicked him in the side. "Now get the fuck out of my club before I gut you like a fish."

He scrambled to his feet, his eyes narrowed into slits and the vein at his temple pulsing hard. "You're going to regret this. My family will—"

"Do nothing," I interrupted, flinging open the door to the bathroom. "Even I know you're on their shit list. That's why you're here instead of at the two-bit strip club the DiTonnos run. If I tell them you attacked Carmela Trassato, you'll be peddling drugs on the corner to support yourself."

His shoulders slumped, and he backed up, halting right outside the threshold. "Rocco deserved what he got. He screwed with my brother's woman. I don't care if they were broken up. Rocco knew better. They were friends. Dominick and Alesio passed the whole thing off as a misunderstanding, except they fucked up. I know the truth and I'm not the only one."

The color leached from Carmela's face, making her ruby-colored lips stand out in sharp relief. She teetered to the side, clutching the bathroom sink basin to steady herself.

"What are you talking about? Rocco never met your brother, and he would never…" Her head swung from side to side. "He wasn't like that. We were—"

"Engaged. I know." Renzo swiped the back of his hand down his neck, smearing the blood onto the front of his gray shirt. "Everyone knows your story. You were marrying him at the end of the month. You'd been engaged for years. You'd dated since high school. The union between you and Rocco was a big fucking deal. Your family had spent thousands of dollars on the wedding. Dominick and your dad had all these plans for Rocco. I get all that."

"So what are you saying?" Her voice trembled and tears tracked down her cheeks.

Renzo's eyes morphed into razor-like slits. "You don't know shit about your family, do you?"

"I-I—"

"Your family lies about everything!" he roared. "Ask them what your precious Rocco was up to before he died. Your brother knows everything."

I flagged a couple of guys working security who had gathered at the end of the hall. "Escort Renzo DiTonno out of here and remove his name from the VIP list."

Renzo lifted his hands next to his head. "I'm done with this place now that you're welcoming the Trassatos in here. I can show myself out."

I watched until he disappeared around the corner.

"You okay?" I said, closing and locking us in the bathroom. Clearly she wasn't. She looked white as a sheet. Her whole body hung like a limp rag and mascara spread out from her eyes like a spider web.

Carmela covered her face with her hands. "I don't know."

"Do you want to talk about it?"

"Not really. No. I want to go home."

I pulled her hands away from her face, and she squeezed her eyes closed. "Look at me." She shook her head. "Carmela, come on."

"I can't talk about Rocco, okay? Whenever someone says his name, I feel like someone stabbed me in the chest." A sob poured from her mouth. "Oh, God. Here it comes again." She opened her eyes and wiped the back of her hand across her face. "Look at me. Why am I crying? I'm such an idiot."

"No, you're not. You loved him. I get it. I may be a callous asshole, but I'm not blind."

"When I think about the last time I saw him, I can't breathe. I said all the wrong things. I wish I could go back in time and have a do over."

"It wouldn't change anything." I rubbed my hands up and down her upper arms. "I'm sure he knew how you felt about him."

"Maybe. Maybe not. We'd been fighting a lot. We were both stressed about the wedding, and we didn't part on good terms. It's hard living with regrets. They eat me alive, even on good days, they find a way to sneak into my thoughts and steal my happiness."

"What happened?"

"Stupid stuff. Meaningless stuff. Nothing that wouldn't have been sorted out the next day, except the next day, he was in a coma, and he was gone shortly after that."

"Then forget that night and focus on the other stuff."

She dropped her head against my shoulder. "I wish I could erase it from my memory."

"I know exactly what you mean." I wasn't lying. My last few months with Laney had been a nightmare. She gotten lost in my world and by the time I realized how far gone she was, it was too late. I didn't recognize her when I saw her around Christmas. She looked like a shell of her former self.

"Why are you being so nice to me?"

Her lips moved against my neck, and her arms slipped around my waist. For the first time, I realized how close we were. When I kissed her at the blackjack table, it'd all been for show. I was more concerned with the guys in the room keeping their hands off her than enjoying the feel of her lips against mine. Not that it worked. That punk ass Renzo didn't hesitate to corner her in the bathroom the first chance he got.

Admittedly, I had kissed her partly because I'd wanted her for longer than I cared to admit out loud. She'd caught my attention a long time before that night my dad and I showed up at her parents' house. I saw her at a restaurant with Rocco a year or so before he died. Then off and on when I covertly checked in on my sister. Carmela was off limits then, and if I were thinking clearly, I would keep her firmly planted in the no-go zone. My dad would have us married within the month if I gave him the smallest opening, and I couldn't risk dragging anyone else into my screwed up life.

"I don't know," I rasped out, finally answering her question because I'm not always as big of an asshole as I make myself out to be.

Despite all of the compelling reasons to stay away from Carmela, I was already talking myself into pushing the boundaries if only this once. I wanted to know what her skin felt like beneath my fingertips and against me. I wanted to know what she tasted like, the sounds she made when she came apart, and so much more. It would take me hours to list the things I wanted to know about Carmela Trassato. Once the thought took root, it wouldn't release its grip on me, and I succumbed to the urge to check a few things off the list.

Shifting closer to her, I framed her lower back with my fingers, mapping that stunning arc where her small waist swelled into her shapely ass. If she wanted me to leave her alone, I would without hesitation. Growing up with a single mom and a sister made me sensitive to forcing myself on a woman or making them uncomfortable.

I waited and watched…

Her eyelids lowered. Her breathing accelerated. Her hands cupped the side of my head and she slanted into me. Without words, she told me everything I needed to know. I pressed my mouth against her full wine-colored lips that somehow managed to be ten times headier than the drink they emulated.

Her lips quivered, her breath hitched, and her muscles tensed. She melded into me, her palms sliding down my face, traveling against the grain of my stubble and finally curling into the ends of my hair. She tugged on the roots, opened her mouth, and I was in. Her tongue twirled around mine, hungry and insistent. I tasted mint. I smelled lemons. I nipped at her lower lip, then pulled it into my mouth. Her breath sputtered. Her body trembled, and for the first time in years, I felt alive. More than alive.

My hands rounded her ass and skirted under the hem of her dress. Her skin was like silk under the pads of my fingers. Her flesh pebbled. Her heart pounded against my chest. A half-sigh, half-moan tumbled from her lips, and instead of checking things off my list and moving on with my life, every reaction only added to my drive to know more about this woman.

Her submission didn't last long enough to quench my thirst. The second my fingers made contact with the lacy edge of her panties, she unwound her arms and retreated a few steps. Breathing roughly with her tits heaving, she trained her unfocused eyes on the floor.

"I think it'd be best if we skipped dinner," she announced after more than a few painfully silent beats.

"We still have plenty of time until our reservation."

"No. I need some space. In fact, we both do. Things got a little out of hand and we're supposed to be finding a way out of the deal we made, not exploring each other."

"I never promised anything."

56

"No. You're right. You didn't." She swallowed and her slim neck bobbed like she had difficulty completing the action. "Except the news of us will inevitably trickle back to Nico, and he won't be happy. I think we should be a little more careful until we're sure which way this will go."

"I don't give a shit about Nico." The quicker the news of Carmela and me made it back to him, the quicker I could unwind this mess my dad concocted. If Nico found out, he'd want to make a deal that kept me far away from Carmela. Undoubtedly, marrying Carmela played a key role in his goal to secure more power in the Trassato family.

"Well, I do. I don't like to hurt people, and Nico will think I'm playing with him if he finds out that we," she waved her hand between us, "you know, and then there's Rocco."

Anger flared through me, eating at my gut. I pounded the palm of my hand against the wall and she recoiled. Here she was worried about Nico while my taste was still fresh on her lips. With nearly a hundred percent certainty, I knew Nico didn't give a shit about Carmela beyond what she could offer him. He manipulated people and situations. He was a treasonous bastard. Everybody realized this except the Trassato family.

As for the Rocco comment, I couldn't touch it. One, you couldn't compete with a dead man's memory. And two, Renzo had insinuated Rocco didn't have a fucking halo over his head the entire time he'd been with Carmela. None of that was my business and nothing good would come of digging up dirt on Rocco except a shitload of hurt feelings that might never be resolved.

"You better get used to it because if this whole thing is going to work, Nico needs to have a pretty strong incentive to cut a deal that satisfies my dad."

"You *want* Nico to find out about us?"

"Of course. What do you think this is about? He wants to marry you, and I'm pretty sure he's our ticket out of this. He'll fight for you. I know it. He needs you, or at least he thinks he does."

"I don't like it. It doesn't feel right."

"And marrying me does?"

"There has to be another way," she whispered, looking lost.

"If you find one, I'm all ears. Until then, incentivizing Nico is our best option."

She shifted on her feet and blew out a shaky breath. "Then why'd you kiss me? Nobody is here to witness it."

I scanned her body from head to toe, letting her see how beautiful I thought she was. "While I might not want to marry you, I'm not blind. You're sexy as fuck, and you know we have chemistry. There's no harm in exploring it. We might as well get it out of our system before you're permanently chained to Nico."

"Ugh. I can't believe you." She cocked her hip and lifted her chin. "I've had enough for tonight. Take me home."

"Sure, *solnyshka*."

Her eyes narrowed. "What does that mean? You said it earlier."

"It's not important."

CHAPTER EIGHT

Carmela

"You're quiet tonight. Is something wrong?"

Nico lifted the bottle of wine and refilled my glass. When he'd invited me to dinner, I didn't realize he planned to have me come to his home. I would have picked a more public venue. I wasn't ready to take our relationship to a new, more intimate level. My instincts told me Nico had every intention of hitting the fast forward button, and tonight was only the beginning of his campaign.

He had pulled out all the stops. Flickering candles, dimmed lighting, red roses, bubbly lasagna, a bottle of Chianti, tiramisu from Carbone's Bakery, soft music.

None of his efforts inspired a surge of fuzzy romantic feelings for him, which didn't make sense. Most women would be floating on a cloud of bliss, having a man like Nico trying to woo them. I wasn't most women, though, and his actions coupled with my mom's insistence on beating the "Nico's so great drum" sent me into a mental tailspin. Their expectations and the inevitability of my future felt like a hangman's noose slowly contracting around my neck.

I lifted the glass of wine to my lips and the tang of tart cherries curled up my nose. I wasn't a big red wine drinker. It made me tired and gave me a dull morning after headache. I poured a drop of the dry wine between my lips. "I'm tired."

"Oh really?"

"I didn't get much sleep."

"Hm." He leaned forward, his forearm skating on top of the table. "Did you get home late last night?"

"Not too late."

"Your mom said you went out to dinner with a friend from school or something. I didn't realize you were taking classes."

"Oh, yeah." I twisted the napkin in my lap. I hated lying, and as much as Kon wanted Nico to think there was something happening between us, I couldn't deal with the fallout tonight. I wasn't strong enough to face Nico or my family. "I'm not taking classes. Not now, anyway. I was working on my interior design degree before everything happened with Rocco, and I haven't found the time to dedicate to it with my dad and everything else."

He reached across the table, brushing his fingertips across the top of my hand. "You want to finish your degree?"

"I do. I enrolled in some classes this fall, and if my mom is doing better, I intend to go ahead with it."

"Rocco and your dad approved of you pursuing a

career?"

"They knew I wanted to finish my degree," I prevaricated, not interested in rehashing the fights about wanting a career. Initially, Rocco supported me. He went so far as to help me put my application together. My dad was a different story altogether. He hated the idea of his daughter being "a lackey" for people too lazy or dumb to pick out their own shit.

Over time, Rocco changed his tune too. He said I could finish my degree if I didn't try to pursue a career, and there was the crux of our nonstop fights leading up to his death. Rocco got this hair up his ass that he wanted to start a family right away and became more and more insistent that I give up my dreams in order to facilitate his.

"Don't you think you're a little too old to finish now?"

If I was bristling before, now my mood bordered on livid. Holy hell. Why did everyone act like I was ancient? I wasn't some spinster who'd spent my life with my nose buried in books. I had come within one month of marrying Rocco. I had plenty of friends and an active social life before my life spiraled into the toilet. I'd been in a funk for three years now, but if I focused on meeting my career goals, I'd find normalcy again, or some version of it.

"No. I don't." I dropped my fork, and it clattered against my plate. "I need twenty credits to finish my degree, which means by next summer I'll be done. I won't even be thirty by then. That hardly qualifies as too old to start a career."

He scooted his chair closer to mine. "Carmela, I didn't mean to imply anything. I support you in whatever you want to do with your life. I'm here for you. I'll always support you to the best of my abilities."

"Okaaay." I drew out the word. "What are you trying to say?"

"While we haven't discussed it, you know your family wants us to get married. I've been attracted to you for a long time. I never did anything about it seeing that you had Rocco. Now that he's gone and your dad isn't around to look after you—"

"I have Gian, and this isn't the Dark Ages. I can take care of myself, get a job and earn money. I don't need to rely on a man to do it for me, and I certainly don't need to marry to find worth or value in my life."

"I know. I don't doubt you're capable of running your life." He twirled the stem of his wine glass, his blue eyes hooded. "Still, you know how things work in our world. You can't be alone, and I gave your father my word that I'd look after you. I take all of my promises seriously."

"So what are you suggesting?"

"We're going to get married. That's not in doubt. Dominick agrees. It's what your father wanted. So we're going to take some time to get to know each other, and see how we can make this work. Once we figure it out, we'll announce our engagement. I'll give you enough freedom to pursue your interests, and I'll pursue mine. We'll make a great team, and we won't step on each other's toes."

Ice rushed down my spine, and I balled my

hands into fists, the sharp bite of my nails the only thing stopping me from throwing wine at his all too smug face. This was like déjà vu. I had two men playing this *let's get to know each other* game and neither one cared about me. The real me. They wanted me for my connections to Dominick. I was a box to be checked on the road to their success.

"So you're basically admitting you aren't interested in me beyond what the connection to my family will provide. I can do what I want and you do whatever it is you do without interference."

"Don't get upset. I like you, Carmela. You're a beautiful, and by most accounts intelligent, woman." His lazy stare dropped to my chest, lingering there for a beat and then swept back up to my face. "I have every intention treating you like a real wife. I want kids. I want to make this work."

"What if we're not compatible? Do you still want to marry me?"

"We'll be compatible."

"You don't know that," I whispered, feeling as if an invisible hand was squeezing my lungs.

"I'll pay for the rest of your degree. I'll make sure you get the job of your dreams when you finish. You can redecorate my place in the meantime to get your creative juices flowing. Do whatever you want. Make it a real home for us, one you're proud of."

"What do you want in return?"

"Your loyalty."

"Do I get yours?"

I saw how the men affiliated with the *family* worked. They put their wives and families on a pedestal, lavished them with material goods. They did put them first, only they had a tendency to stray.

Without question, my mom and dad loved each other. I was aware of the rumors, though, and they weren't reassuring. I overheard the hushed accusations my mom threw his way when my dad came home late reeking of cheap perfume. I didn't understand how she put up with it. It was one of the reasons I loved Rocco so much. We were a team. He didn't keep secrets from me, and I never had to worry about him cheating on me.

Renzo DiTonno's rant floated through my head not for the first time since my disastrous pseudo-date with Kon. His accusation, coupled with kissing Kon, made sleeping last night next to impossible, and I still couldn't decide which event had rattled me more.

"Of course. You'd be my wife."

"Are loyalty and fidelity one and the same?" I probed, needing to understand the type of arrangement he was proposing.

He took a deep drink of his wine, nearly draining the glass. "It's what we should strive for, but both of us are old enough to know that nothing lasts forever. There's no such thing as a happy ending, Carmela. Not with Rocco. Not with me, or anyone else for that matter. Every relationship has its ups and downs. Ours won't be any different."

I clutched the seat of my chair with both hands. My already absent appetite shriveled up died, and I wanted to go home. "I can't fault you for being honest. I guess I have a lot to think about."

He stared at me without explaining or

contradicting me, and for the first time, I noticed that the music had stopped. Maybe he turned it off at some point or maybe it was life's way of confirming fairytales didn't exist. While things may appear perfect on the outside, more often than not they concealed secrets and a whole lot of ugliness.

Not a minute too soon his doorbell rang and my shoulders sagged with relief. The tension stretching between us had thickened to the point where I didn't feel like I could take in another breath.

"Excuse me. I should get that." He pushed back his chair and crossed the room, his polished black Ferragamos clipping over the hardwood floors.

The door squeaked open. Lowered voices floated down the hall. One of them was a woman, piquing my curiosity. Nico and I weren't anything to each other. Not yet anyway. Sure, we were in the middle of negotiating our potential marriage and we'd kissed at Gian and Evie's wedding, though in spite of all of that, I didn't believe for a second either of those things would keep Nico from playing the field. At this point, I truly didn't care either way. After we married was another story. I didn't want his infidelities waved in my face. I wouldn't spend my life playing the tragic wife role.

I padded down the hall, freezing with one foot suspended in front of the other. "Ava, what are you doing here?"

"There you are." She took a step back, dropping her hand from Nico's upper arm. Her gaze darted to Nico, then back to me. "I was looking for you."

"Why's that?"

She yanked on the hem of her black midriff-baring shirt. "Your mom said you were here and I was in the neighborhood, so I thought I'd stop by and see if you needed a ride."

"Thanks for thinking of me. You shouldn't have bothered, though. Nico can take me home or I'll catch a cab."

"Oh, well, I should get going then." She twisted her honey colored hair around her finger. I didn't understand why she lightened it. It was so pretty and soft before she started playing with it. "Tell your mom I said hi."

"Don't be silly. Come in and have a drink with us. We were finishing up with dinner. You can share our dessert."

Nico shot me a dark look, and I smiled blandly. I wasn't anxious to get back to our conversation. I couldn't promise Nico a future right now. I had to come to an agreement with Kon and his father before I could move forward with Nico, and I wasn't sure I wanted to spend the rest of my life with him. Outwardly, he had several of the things women yearned for in a man: a lean athletic build, a swoon-worthy face, money, and power. Only I wanted more—a deeper connection. I wanted to share some level of affection and trust with the man I married even if it never amounted to love.

"I don't want to intrude." Ava kept her brown eyes trained on Nico rather than me. "I'm sure Nico has all sorts of things planned tonight."

"No, come in," Nico gritted out, opening the door wider. While his gesture was welcoming, his voice was unforgiving and terse, leaving little doubt he didn't like her barging in on our dinner.

Ava swallowed hard, then glanced over her shoulder. "No. I need to get going. I have early morning plans."

"Oh. Okay. Well, call me soon and we'll go out for dinner or drinks sometime next week."

"Sure thing."

Nico closed the door the minute she turned her back.

"That was strange. Has she been here before or something?"

"Yeah, most likely." Nico draped his arm over my shoulder and ushered me to the dinner table. "Ava and my sister Gemma were best friends back in the day. They don't hang out much anymore. Gemma got caught up in a bad scene. Drugs, parties, booze. She's cleaned up her act and has a sobriety buddy, Lanelle or something. They seem to be keeping each other outta trouble. That's all I care about. Her son needs her."

I shifted on my feet, uncomfortable with the mention of his sister. Gemma had become somewhat of a taboo subject in the past few years. Everyone pretended like she didn't exist.

"Yeah, and I'm sure Ava wouldn't forget where you lived. I think she has quite the crush on you," I said, trying to change the subject.

He rubbed the back of his neck, and his face hardened. "She's talked about me to you? What'd she say?"

"Nothing unflattering." I forced out a stilted chuckle. Despite the fact that Ava got on my nerves sometimes, I owed her my loyalty. That's the way my family worked. "I don't think she's a stalker or anything if that's what you're worried about."

"No, of course not. Forget I said anything. I don't want to talk about them. Do you want some dessert or coffee?"

I surveyed our abandoned dinner. Nothing appealed to me anymore. I came here with good intentions. I wanted to see if Nico and I were compatible, and while I didn't hate him, I wasn't attracted to him either. Unlike Kon, he didn't make my stomach flutter with a crooked smile or a brush of his hand. I needed to get over my fascination with Kon. It was stupid and dangerous.

"No. I'm pretty tired. Can we finish our discussion later? I don't feel so great. I think I'm coming down with something."

It wasn't entirely a lie. I *was* coming down with something. It was called a guilty conscience from putting myself in this position. Cutting a deal with Alix and Kon Trincher was my first mistake. My second was being too weak to refuse my father's dying request to marry Nico.

I skirted around him, heading to the door. Nico's hand circled my forearm, applying enough pressure to get my attention. The muscle in his jaw twitched. His eyes bored into me, and my heart sped up, and not in a good way. For the first time in my life, Nico DeAngelo scared the crap out of me. I'd heard the rumors. He was ruthless. He had a trigger-happy finger. He never negotiated. I'd never seen this side of him, and it spooked me.

"This conversation is not over. We *will* get married. I gave your father my word. Dominick expects it to happen sooner rather than later. I don't like to disappoint people."

My mouth went dry and I licked my lips, searching for the right response. "Give me time."

"I'm not a patient man, Carmela."

I peeled his fingers from my arm. "And I don't like to be pushed around."

Our gazes locked in battle. Time slowed. Tension built, multiplying until I couldn't breathe a single molecule of oxygen into my lungs. After what felt like hours, a smile spread across Nico's face. "That's why I like you." He kissed the corner of my mouth. "We're going to be good together. You'll see."

CHAPTER NINE

Konstantin

"I heard you took the Trassato chick to the club a couple of nights ago."

My spine snapped to attention even though my dad's comment didn't surprise me. I expected him to hear every little detail about my guest, which would lead to him spending a good half hour analyzing the video from the night. At least he kept the recording devices out of the bathroom. I didn't have any interest in explaining what happened with Carmela after the encounter with Renzo.

"Of course I did." Running my index finger along the hood of a red Porsche 911, I lifted one shoulder like I didn't have a care in the world, and continued analyzing the cars in the warehouse. "You've been begging me to make a move for months."

His chocolate brown loafers clicked over the oil-stained concrete floor. "I thought I'd have to set up a date myself."

"I told you I'd get the Trassatos to give us access to their territories, and that's precisely what I'm doing."

"So did you decide to go the engagement route?"

"I'm working a couple of different angles." I climbed into the car. The new car odor clung to the leather. I checked the mileage. Four thousand. It would sell for good money in Russia. "You don't need to worry about it. I'll seal the deal within the next few months."

"Good. Good." He combed his fingers through his faded red hair, his eyes never breaking contact with mine. "By the way, a few guys from the DiTonno family will be here in the next fifteen minutes."

"Why the fuck are they coming here?"

"I invited them. I think it's time to renegotiate our business arrangement."

I got out of the car and flung the door closed. It echoed loudly in the high-ceilinged building. "Why would they agree to that?"

"My daughter married Gian. You're close with Carmela. An alliance would cut the DiTonnos off at the knees. I wouldn't need them anymore, and they'd need me more than ever. They make nearly a quarter of a million dollars a month from our mutual business interests. More when we have a shipment of women."

I gritted my teeth. I'd told my dad hundreds of times I didn't want anything to do with human trafficking. It disgusted me. He didn't give a shit thanks to it having a high profit margin. He recruited the majority of women from the Ukraine

71

and Romania because those countries didn't have many job prospects regardless of their education level.

He posted advertisements promising big money and free housing for nannies, dancers, or waitresses in the U.S. He paid for their transportation and provided the proper travel papers. When they arrived, he subdued them and forced them into a life of prostitution by stripping them of their identification and drugging them until they became addicts. In the meantime, they were stowed in a crap ass, shady hotel and raped ten times a day until they went crazy or overdosed.

Thinking about it made me fucking sick.

When I discovered the full extent of his involvement, I refused to be drawn in any further. Needless to say, after a huge fight, we came to an arrangement that suited us both. He recruited the DiTonnos, and I concentrated on managing the gambling activities and our car export business.

My dad had opened my eyes to a world drastically different from my hometown in Nebraska. Part of me was thankful I had so many opportunities. I had more money than I could spend in this lifetime. I owned multiple homes. I paid off my mom's hobby farm and bought her the building where she operated her dance studio.

The other part of me hated he'd exposed me to the shadowy underbelly of organized crime at such a young age. Life would have been simpler. I could have gone my entire life without knowing how drugs traveled the globe and how weapons made it into the hands of dictators and terrorists despite embargos and laws to the contrary.

"So you plan to rope the Trassatos into your side of the business?"

"Why the hell not? Nico and Dominick are first and foremost businessmen. Once they see the numbers, they won't be able to resist, and they have more power and territories than the DiTonnos. It'll be a win-win."

"Just so ya know, I don't want anything to do with the transport of *girls*. I don't want to hear about it, I don't want to see it, and I sure as fuck don't want to negotiate the terms."

"Jesus fucking Christ, Kon, this isn't about the *girls*. You know I only do that once or twice a year. It's a big payout, but I have to grease too many hands and there's a shitload of paperwork. It's a lot of work for an old man. There are easier ways to make money these days."

"I'd rather we stayed the hell away from that kind of work," I grumbled.

"You act like I don't have feelings. That's not close to true. I'm not fucking Stalin and I'm no saint either. I do what I have to do to because when you lead a life like mine where someone's always itching to take your spot or eliminate you, you have to scrape, kill, and outsmart your rivals or you might as well dig your own grave."

"If not for the girls, why did you invite them here?"

"I want to renegotiate how much protection money we pay them to keep people away from this warehouse."

"They won't agree. We've gone down this road

with them before."

Currently, we paid them five percent on every car we sold in Russia. Basically, we had guys stealing cars all over the DiTonno controlled territory. They delivered them to our warehouse and we shipped them out less than twenty-four hours later, stuffed inside crates lined with mattresses and labeled as ordinary household goods.

The DiTonnos had decades of infrastructure and connections that we didn't, including port authorities and police officers, so we paid the DiTonnos to keep everyone off our backs. In turn, they did what was necessary to make sure all the appropriate authorities looked the other way. They were the whores of the Italian mafia. They'd do anything to make a buck, unlike the Trassatos, who pretended they had honor and morals.

"Oh," he smiled condescendingly, "they will and they'll do it with a fucking smile."

A knock sounded on the metal door leading to the outside.

"I guess that's them," I said, removing one of the guns from the holster strapped to my chest.

My dad keyed in the code to disarm the alarm and flipped the deadbolt. "Thanks for joining us."

Alesio D'Orizio sauntered into the room, Renzo following closely on his heels. He had two black eyes and a split lip from our confrontation a couple of nights ago.

Anger pulsed through me. My heartbeat kicked up a notch, and I stormed forward, my gun pointed at Renzo. "What the fuck is he doing here?"

Alesio pulled out his gun, aiming it at my chest.

Renzo froze, his hands raised next to his head in the universal sign of surrender. My dad stepped between us, one hand on Alesio's chest on the other on mine.

"What the fuck is this about? We're not here to fight. We're here to discuss business."

"Tell that to your son," Alesio sneered, his dark eyes wild, his jaw muscles twitching. He was one sick fucker, and he'd done more than one stint in the big house. I shouldn't have provoked him. He killed more than his share of people as he climbed the ladder to the job of underboss for the DiTonno family. "What the hell is wrong with him?"

"That punk," I jammed my gun in Renzo's direction, "came into my club a couple of days ago causing a shitload of trouble and harassing one of my guests."

"Renzo, is that true?" Alesio didn't break eye contact with me.

Renzo cleared his throat, and dipped his head against his chest. "It was a misunderstanding. I apologized and agreed not to go back there again. It's all settled. There's no reason for a sit-down."

My dad dropped his hands to his sides, the corners of his eyes crinkling while he squinted at me. "What's this about?"

I lowered my gun, stuffing it back into the holster hidden beneath my leather jacket. "He accosted Carmela Trassato in the bathroom, spewing all kinds of crap."

"What the fuck was going through your head?" Alesio shoved his gun into the waistband of his pants. "We finally put that shit with the Trassatos behind us, and now you're stirring the pot again. If Gian hears you harassed his sister, he's going to be gunning for us again."

Renzo backpedaled, his hands buried deep in the pockets of his black suit. I had no clue why the Italians felt the need to walk around like they were a bunch of pretentious bankers instead of seedy criminals like the rest of us.

"I know. Like I said, it was a misunderstanding. I was shitfaced. All that crap with the Trassatos came rushing back to me, and I acted like an ass."

"That business between your brother and Rocco is over. I don't want to hear about it again or you will be *broken*. You understand? I don't care who was fucking who, who got who pregnant, or who threw the first punch. It doesn't matter. It was buried with your brother and Rocco, and that's where it needs to stay."

"Got it," Renzo said through gritted teeth. "It won't happen again."

A few tense moments passed with them eyeballing each other, presumably communicating silently.

Alesio cleared his throat. "So, Alix, why'd you call this meeting?"

"I think it's time to renegotiate the DiTonnos' cut of the car exports. We agreed to five percent a year ago. It was a fair deal for both of us back when the profits were lower and the business model wasn't proven. Now, however, the business has grown and the risk has decreased. We think two point five percent would be more in line with the services you're providing."

Alesio's shoulders snapped back and his hands flexed. "You want to cut our share in half?"

"Yeah, I do." My dad's smile curled up his face like a snake soaking up a little sunlight. "But it's your choice. I could negotiate something with the Trassatos. I'm sure you heard about my daughter marrying Gian, and you already heard how close Kon is with Carmela. They're practically family, whereas you guys are simply business partners. I know if I bring this opportunity to them, they'll treat me right."

Alesio's fingers twitched at his sides and his eyes narrowed, calculating his next move. Renzo's head seesawed. My dad's smile stretched wider until he resembled a macabre jack-o-lantern. He thrived on danger and confrontation, loving it almost as much as the power and money.

The air conditioning unit hummed. A tiny plumbing leak struck a steady *drip, drip, drip*. The air churned with enough testosterone to supply twenty men. Alesio lifted his hand, making a move toward his gun.

"Don't even think about it," I snarled, pulling a gun from each side of my holster. There were a lot of rumors about me, some true and some false. My ability to shoot with either hand was true. I'd mastered it the summer I turned sixteen. I could take out both Alesio and Renzo before either of them could blink, much less get off a shot. I was that good. "We get into a shootout and neither of you will be walking out of here alive."

"Fucking hell," Alesio cursed. "The boss is not going to like it if I bend over and agree to half our profits."

"He doesn't have to like it," I snapped. "He has to accept it or we'll put out feelers for more cooperative business partners. I'm sure we'll have more than a few takers."

"Four percent," Alesio countered. "With an option to reconsider in a year."

"Three percent," I said, jabbing the muzzle of my gun toward him.

"Three and a half."

"Done," Alix interjected. "The new percentage will be effective immediately."

Grinning, I stuffed my guns back into the hostler. "As always, it was good doing business with you. Now get out of my face. I have shit to do to make sure the latest shipment sets sail tomorrow."

"What about our other deals?" Alesio prodded.

My dad flipped the lock and opened the door. "Right now they're fine. If anything changes, Kon or I will be in touch."

CHAPTER TEN

Carmela

I added some links to my proposal, reread my client's preferences, and clicked send on the email. My online interior design business didn't make much money, maybe one to three thousand dollars a month. I didn't care, though. It gave me independence and something of my own.

Right after Rocco died, I dropped out of interior design school. I had missed weeks of school sitting by his bedside hoping and praying he'd wake up, only he never did. Eventually, his parents decided to remove life support.

I had fought for more time. A month, a week, anything. I'd be lying if I claimed I didn't resent their decision at the time, despite the fact his scan showed minimal brain function. None of that mattered to me. I held out hope for a miracle. I wanted to have one more hour with him, so I could apologize, tell him I loved him, and kiss him like I meant it. I guess it made me selfish for wanting him back if only to clear my conscience and give us a less ugly ending.

He died within hours of removing life support. I grieved, I raged, I sulked. And after months of hopelessness, I started an online business where people could send me pictures of the room they wanted to redecorate, as well as a link to a Pinterest board documenting the things they loved and room dimensions.

For three to five hundred dollars, I would provide design options complete with paint colors and links to furniture that worked for their room. All of it was done anonymously so the work couldn't be traced back to my family and me. I went to the coffee shop near the apartment where I lived before my dad died three times a week and worked, emailing proposals and researching trends.

The metal chair next to me scraped on the floor, diverting my attention from the computer screen in front of me.

"You're a hard woman to get a hold of."

"Konstantin?" I shut my laptop and glanced at the door. Evie said she might meet me here after her rehearsal. She'd landed the lead role in a new production, and she was dying to tell me about it now that she had returned from her honeymoon with Gian. "What are you doing here?"

"What do you think?"

He set a mug of coffee onto the table and settled into the chair. His clear blue eyes drilled into me as if he was cataloging my features. He shifted his body to face me, his jean-clad thighs brushing against my bare legs. While we were barely touching, I felt him everywhere.

"I didn't invite you, so honestly, I have no idea."

The corners of his lips quirked up like he found me entirely too amusing for my comfort. I wasn't stupid. I knew why he was here. I'd been dodging his calls and texts for nearly a week. After our seriously, judgment-impaired kiss and the weird business relationship marriage proposal from Nico, I needed space from both of them. I felt like a commodity rather than a person, and I didn't like it. Not one bit.

"Don't play games. You're avoiding me."

He slid one arm over the back of my chair, his thumb brushing my neck beneath the fall of my hair. My lungs drew in the leather of his jacket mixed with the woodsy scent of his soap. Mini-sparks shot down my spine. Desire pulsed through me, roaming free and wild like it'd been suppressed for too long. My mind seized as I processed the sensation.

Oh hell no. Not this again.

I focused on the floor to ceiling windows in front of me, desperately searching for Evie's telltale strawberry blonde hair. Now close to lunchtime, throngs of umbrella-wielding people filled the street. Pregnant gray clouds hovered over the skyline. It was going to rain. My feet itched with the need to hit the pavement and splash in the puddles like I did with Gian and Rocco when we were kids.

As silly as it sounded, I loved walking in the rain. It washed away the dirt and sins of the city like the symbolic dunk in the baptismal basin. The smell, so clean and pure, was unlike anything in the world.

"It's only been a week," I answered, glancing at my watch. Evie's rehearsal ended nearly an hour ago. She could walk in the door any minute, and I'd have a clusterfuck of the first order on my hands. "We can do something tonight. Meet me at The Salty Fork for dinner. I haven't been there yet. Surely you can snag us reservations. Text me the time and I'll meet you there."

I started packing away my belongings, hoping he'd get the hint I wanted him to leave. When I finished, I chugged the last of my coffee and checked my phone.

"A week," he mused, tapping me on the shoulder with his tatted finger, and completely ignoring all my attempts to get rid of him. "That's seven days too many. This whole thing has been hanging over our heads for over a year. I'd like to get my life back as soon as possible. Wouldn't you?"

"What's the point?" I shrugged. "If you haven't noticed, I'm kind of boxed in here. I end up with you or I do my family's bidding and marry Nico. Neither of which appeal to me. I'm in no rush."

"You could have refused my dad's offer."

"You're right, I could have, only I'm not that cold-blooded. I wanted to help your sister and my brother."

I turned to the front window again for the sixth time in the last minute or two. Kon probably assumed I had a nervous tic. I spotted Evie standing across the street. She pulled her phone out of her pocket and pressed it to her ear.

Not good. So not good.

Without a doubt, I looked more than a little unhinged. My eyes were as wild as the chaotic drum of my heart. When I envisioned how this whole thing with Kon would work, I never progressed beyond feeling sorry for myself and wondering how I'd get out of it. The impending confrontation with Evie crammed the cold hard reality in my face.

My brother would freak. Like go on a murderous rampage freak. And Evie…well, she only mentioned her brother once in the last year, and it was to affirmatively state she never wanted to see him again. That he was a lying, traitorous piece of crap. In hindsight, I should have pled his case a little and let her in on the secret that he was instrumental in getting her sociopathic dad to back off and consent to their relationship without using it to his advantage.

I popped out of my seat like a jack-in-the-box.

"What's wrong?" Kon said.

"Evie's here," I hissed.

"Evie," he parroted, his gaze leaping to the front window. "What the hell is she doing here?"

"Meeting me."

"Why?"

"We're friends. She's my sister-in-law, or did you forget?"

"Why didn't you say something?"

"If you didn't notice, I was trying to get rid of you."

"Yeah, I noticed." He rubbed his knuckles across his jaw, his shirt stretching across the contours of his chest. "All the same, you could have clued me into the exact reason *why* you wanted me to leave."

"How did you find me here anyway?"

"I have my ways." His body tensed for a beat, then a huge smile slid across his face.

"Well, do me a favor and disappear, like right now."

He took his sweet freaking time lumbering from the chair, and I curled my hands into the hem of my shirt to prevent myself from succumbing to the urge to push him across the room.

"So I'll see you tonight?"

"What are you doing? Go, get out of here," I snapped, my teeth clenched, and my hands balled into fists.

"Are you afraid of my sister?"

"No, but I am afraid of my entire family figuring out that we're doing *whatever*."

"No matter how this plays out, your family's gonna find out about us." He tucked a strand of hair behind my ear and his hand lingered near my neck. "You understand that, right, *solnyshka*?"

"Not yet, please. I need a little more time to figure things out."

"It's better to rip off the bandage and get it over with. Don't you agree?"

My eyes latched onto his ocean blue ones, secrets and mischief dancing right beneath the surface. I couldn't look away. My lungs constricted and my palms were sweaty.

He bent his head until his lips brushed the shell of my ear, and his fingers slid up my neck, cradling the back of my head. Chills danced down my arms. "Relax. Everything's going to be fine. You'll see. I'm not going to let anyone hurt you."

84

"Carmela, I can't believe you didn't tell me your news when we talked this morning," Evie said, flinging open the door. She stared at her phone with a huge grin on her face, still ignorant to the metaphorical bomb about to explode.

His voice velvety as honey yet cold as ice, Kon said, "Evie, it's been a long time."

Her mouth opened and closed in quick succession. She shook her head as if she couldn't believe her eyes. "Carmela," she said, her voice ragged and her face paper white. "What's he doing here with you?"

His hand flexed on the back of my head, signaling me not to respond. "Carmela and I are…friends. Isn't that right?"

"Friends?" Squinting until I could no longer see the whites of her eyes, Evie aimed a shaky finger at Kon. "If this is another one of your tricks to mess with my life—"

"It's not." His hand dropped from my head, and I felt…bereft. Kon glanced at his sister then planted a kiss on my cheek. "I'll text you about later."

He opened the glass door and disappeared into the maze of umbrellas, leaving me to deal with fallout.

"What the hell was that about?" Evie yelled, her voice louder and more confident in her brother's absence. "Please tell me you're not hanging out with Kon. I don't care what he says. I don't trust him."

"Like he said, we're friends, of sorts."

"That doesn't make sense. You don't have anything in common. "

"We met to figure out how to get you and Gian back together." I shrugged, trying to convey a casualness that contradicted my skyrocketing blood pressure and damp brow. "Since then, we've been friendly. Besides, he's your brother, cut him some slack. He can't be as bad as you're imagining. He's always been nice to me."

For the most part, that was true, although I didn't like the way he and his father had backed me into a corner. Admittedly, I could have walked away and let Evie and Gian figure it out themselves. In hindsight, they probably would've ended up together regardless of what I did. They were meant to be together. Even jaded and emotionally wounded, I could see that.

"I can't forgive him."

"You used to be close. You talked about him all the time even though you hadn't seen him in years."

"I don't know much about him anymore except that he's a different person than when we were kids." Her brown eyes clouded for a second, and she swallowed hard. "There's nothing happening between you two, right?"

I wanted to tell her no, only I couldn't. I didn't know what would happen between us down the road, and like Kon said, I might as well get the hard stuff over with. "It's complicated. You don't need to worry, though, I know it's not going anywhere."

I cringed at my words. I couldn't promise that. Admittedly, Kon wanted out of this arrangement as much as I did, but that didn't mean anything. Nico's reaction wasn't a sure thing. He didn't love me or feel all that passionate toward me. Our limited kisses could only be described as friendly and not all that attention grabbing. He might lose all interest in me once he found out about Kon.

"Wow, um, okay." She tugged on the scarf around her neck like she couldn't breathe. "I'm confused. I thought you and Nico were—"

"Nico and I are exploring a possible future, though I don't feel much of anything for him beyond friendship. He goes out of his way to make sure our dates go smoothly. He treats me well. That's all it is right now. Maybe it will change down the line. I can't say for sure."

"Really?" Evie frowned, and her eyebrows snapped together. "Your mom told Gian and I that you and Nico plan to announce your engagement next weekend at Dominick's birthday party."

"What?" My head jerked back like I'd been slapped. If my family and Nico went behind my back and arranged this, I'd lose my mind. "That's news to me."

"Wow. Okay. That's weird. Nico took her to lunch yesterday to sort out the details. She called me on the phone a couple of minutes ago. She told me she was taking you shopping tomorrow for an engagement dress."

A chill darted down my spine, and I swung my head wildly from side to side. "No, I never agreed to any of this. I'm not ready to jump into another relationship. I'm still figuring things out."

"Since you feel something for my brother?" Her face looked like she'd sniffed something repulsive. "I can guarantee he's using you. He has an agenda. He always did, he always will. He's not a nice person. Not anymore. My dad ruined everything good in him."

"People aren't black and white, Evie. You of all people should understand this. My brother isn't a saint by any stretch of the imagination, yet you overlook that because you love him."

"You're not suggesting you're in love with Kon, are you?" Her voice rose an octave or two, and she looked like she was on the verge of having a panic attack with her flared eyes, short, rapid breaths, and clenched hands. People at the nearby tables stared, too interested to pretend they weren't listening. "He's a bastard. He nearly ruined my life. Gian hates him. He does bad stuff. Gian told me a few things, and it's ugly."

I picked up my messenger bag and slung it over my shoulder. "While I'm sure that's true, you don't need to worry about me falling for your brother. My shot at a happily ever after fairytale expired the moment Rocco took his last breath. And let's face it, my family wants me to marry Nico. I probably will at some point seeing that's what everyone expects me to do. It doesn't matter either way. I'm only going through the motions these days."

I clamped my mouth shut. I couldn't say anything else unless I wanted to risk a full breakdown. Every damn time I talked about Rocco, it felt like I was suffocating. I waved and took a few uncoordinated steps toward the exit, feeling lightheaded and sick deep in the pit of my stomach.

"Don't leave." She grabbed my hand. "I didn't mean to upset you. Let's talk about this."

"I can't. Not right now. I've gotta go."

CHAPTER ELEVEN

Konstantin

Sitting in one of the hottest restaurants in the city with an empty seat across from me and an open bottle of sparkling wine was humbling to say the least. I scrolled through my phone and checked for a missed text or voicemail from Carmela. She blew off our dinner date after confirming by text earlier this afternoon. It marked the first time I'd been stood up for a date since high school, and I didn't like it. I'd dressed in my best black suit and tie despite the fact the blue tie felt like a noose around my neck.

When forty minutes had passed and I still hadn't heard a word from her, I had a choice to make. I could stay and make the best of the night or tuck tail and run like a wounded boy. Not wanting to show any weakness or unease, I drank the bottle of wine and ate a small meal instead of storming out of the restaurant. I didn't like people knowing I cared.

All that changed the minute my dad's name

flashed across my phone. I declined it. The third time he called, I answered. I knew better than to press Bloody Alix, as his enemies called him. While he was my flesh and blood, he wouldn't hesitate to put me in my place. Despite the fact he was a fucking prick most of the time, I respected him.

I dropped a couple of hundreds on the table and walked out of the restaurant with the phone next to my ear. "Did you did need something?"

"Konstantin, what the fuck is going on? You said you had this thing with the Trassato chick under control."

"I do. You need to back off and stop micromanaging me. She's a woman, not a business deal. This is going to take a little finesse."

"Yeah, well, you need to alter your strategy right fucking now considering you already managed to make a mess out of this situation. I mean, I fucking handed you Carmela Trassato on a silver platter and you sat on your hands, drowning yourself in booze and whores for the better part of the year."

"Don't push me. I'm not in the mood." I closed my car door a little harder than necessary, enjoying the satisfying *thud*. The engine of my BMW roared and my tires squealed as I sped away from the curb.

"I've got this under control," I growled. "Carmela's on the same page."

He chuckled sarcastically, his taunt echoing in my ears. "You've been played, Kon. Everyone's saying she's announcing her engagement to Nico in less than two weeks at Dominick's house."

Pain sliced through my chest, and I slammed on my brakes. The rear of my car skidded to the side.

My head jerked forward, then backward, hitting the headrest. I didn't say anything for second. I couldn't. Thoughts of Carmela and the way she clung to me at the club banged around in my head along with the skittish way she'd behaved today. He was right. She played me. I rammed the heel of my hand into the dashboard. Fire shot up my arm and my hand throbbed in time with my anger. "How do you know?"

"It's not a secret. Everyone knows. I can't believe you don't. That's all I've heard about for the last two hours. The fucking DiTonnos rubbed it in my face." His voice turned low and threatening. "She made a joke out of us and I don't like it. I won't let this go. I don't give a fuck about the Trassatos or all of their connections. I'm not afraid to take them out. As a matter of a fact, Nico will be the first to go, along with Carmela. We can take care of this at the party."

"We're not doing anything yet. We still have time to sort this out."

I stepped on the gas pedal again, speeding down the street, weaving in and out of traffic and ignoring the honks and angry hand gestures. I had no idea where I was going. I only knew I needed to drive and clear my head.

"I'm done playing games with the Trassatos. They've screwed me over for the last time."

"What the fuck are you suggesting? We storm Dominick's house and get in some sort of gunfight? We don't have the manpower to go head to head with them. You know that. That's why we cut the deal with the DiTonnos last year."

"Fine, then we'll have them help us."

I tightened my grip on the steering wheel until my knuckles whitened. This was a disaster in the making. "Give me a week. That's all I'm asking for. Carmela doesn't want to marry Nico any more than she wants to marry me. I think I can get her to walk this back and buy us some more time to use her as leverage to work out a deal with Nico or Dominick."

His blew out a heavy breath. "Fine. I'll give you a week and not one day more. If she doesn't bend to our will, I'll need time to prepare our next move."

He disconnected the phone before I could respond, and music boomed through my speakers instead of his voice. I powered off my phone, not wanting to hear from anyone else tonight. I had all of the bad news I could take. Everything else would have to wait until my I got my head screwed on right.

Hour after hour passed, and I drove through the streets trying to come up with a plan. While my gut told me Carmela wouldn't intentionally screw me over, I didn't know much about her. My father and I had used her good intentions to our advantage, cornering her until she didn't have any choice but to accept a shitty deal. Unfortunately for us, cornered prey eventually lashed out.

She didn't want to marry Nico, that much was evident. However, given an option between the two of us, she clearly decided he was the better choice. That was fine. I didn't want to marry her either.

Without question, I liked the way her curves felt under my hands and the sensation of her lips gliding against mine. None of those things changed the way I felt about getting involved with a woman for more than a night or two, though. My relationships with Laney and my mom left a sour taste in my mouth and taught me women weren't worth the trouble. They always betrayed you in the end.

For all that, I couldn't explain why I ended my journey two blocks away from the Trassatos' family home. I got out of my car and ambled down the street, my eyes taking in the spaced out homes and big trees complete with tire swings and yard art. If there was something I missed about Nebraska, it was the wide-open spaces where you could breathe clean air and be alone somewhere other than inside your apartment.

My father's years of indoctrination echoed in my ears.

Negotiate from a position of strength, not weakness. Never show anyone you care. Be the first to walk away.

None of those sentiments jived with a trip to the Trassatos' house to confront Carmela in the middle of the fucking night, yet there I was standing on the sidewalk in front of their home like a stalker. If Dominick or Gian heard about this, I'd be as good as dead.

Fuck, my dad would probably kill me himself if he found out. He wanted this union, or more accurately, he wanted to get something out of the threat of a union between Carmela and me. He didn't care if we ever tied the knot. More importantly, though, he didn't want me to alert the Trassatos to a possible counterpunch, which was reason enough to march back to the car and get my ass home. Only I knew I wouldn't stop myself now. I wouldn't be able to sleep until I heard her explanation.

I hopped over the wrought iron fence lining the perimeter of their property. My back pressed to the brick exterior of their home, my breathing ragged. My eyes darted around the manicured lawn, and I listened. Crickets chirped with annoying frequency. The moon looked like a white smudge in the otherwise black sky. A hot, muggy breeze ruffled through my hair and clung to my suit, making me feel damp and sticky.

I scanned the windows above the garage. Based on my research, Carmela inhabited the studio apartment above the three-car garage. I spotted the cracked balcony door, and I knew I had a way into her room. While it would have been better for me if the apartment were isolated, a window-lined hallway connected it to the second story of the house.

A quick examination of the home told me I'd have to scale the nearby tree and dangle like a fucking monkey from the branch until I reached the Romeo and Juliet balcony on the side of the garage. Not my idea of a fun weekend night by any stretch of the imagination. Good thing I spent most of my childhood roaming a farm and doing shit that paled in comparison.

"Go big or go home," I mumbled, scaling the trunk.

The bark dug into the pads of my fingers, making crackling noises that sounded much louder in my head than in reality. When I grasped the branch that nearly brushed against the railing of the balcony, I propelled my legs, swinging one hand in front of the other. I swayed back and forth to gain momentum and launched my body over the top of the black iron railing.

I paused there, catching my breath and checking for any signs Carmela was still awake. I wasn't deluded enough to believe she'd welcome my visit. She didn't show up tonight for a reason. Either she planned to keep on avoiding me, or her brother had forbidden her from seeing me again. Maybe she was sick of the whole thing and ran away. I didn't care about her reasoning. We made a deal, and I felt a little more than irritated that she didn't bother keeping me in the loop.

With one hand on the gun in my suit jacket, I pushed open the door. Listening. Calculating. Darkness greeted me. The minute I stepped over the threshold, a light flashed, blinding me for a second and I squinted. An object *whooshed* through the air. When I opened my eyes, it was already too late.

CHAPTER TWELVE

Carmela

My heart thumping wildly, I aimed my flashlight at the balcony door. The second I saw a blurred black silhouette, I dropped the flashlight, grabbed a nearby lamp, and hefted it over my head. With my eyes pinched shut, I swung as hard as I could. The metal made contact with the person. I stumbled sideways, and the lamp slipped out of my unsteady hands.

The person grunted, and my eyes cracked open, searching for another weapon, but I saw Konstantin Trincher instead.

"What are you doing here?" I said, my voice thick with the remnants of fear.

"Have you lost your fucking mind?" Kon growled, trying to keep his voice down. He looked at me as if I were the crazy one when he had snuck into my room in the middle of the night. What did he expect? That I'd greet him with a warm hug and a big sloppy "thanks for coming I missed you so much" kiss?

"*I'm* not the lunatic here." I pointed at the open balcony door. "You broke into my room in the middle of the night. Did you expect me to cower beneath my sheets and wait for someone to kill me?"

"Yeah, well, you didn't need to hit me in the head," he grumbled, his hand palming the side of the face.

I winced. I didn't want to hurt him. Well, I did before I realized who he was. When I met him a year or so ago, I thought he was a soulless asshole. My opinion evolved into something I couldn't explain the minute he defended me when Renzo cornered me in the bathroom. I didn't hate him, and I didn't particularly *like* him, not entirely. In spite of or perhaps due to my confusing feelings for him, I'd let him kiss me. Touch me. It had been too damn long since I'd been with a man, and even when Rocco and I were together, we never had much time alone. We kissed hello and goodbye, and we only had sex a few times. All said and done, Rocco and I had a mostly unremarkable sex life before he died.

"Are you in pain?"

"What do you think?" He angled the side of his face toward me. It was stained a bright, angry red, and he had a short gash across his upper cheekbone.

Crap, that looked like it hurt.

"I don't think you need stitches, but you're going to have a bruise. Do you want some ice?"

I didn't wait for an answer. I made my way to the kitchenette and grabbed a bag of frozen vegetables from the freezer. By the time I turned around, he was sitting against my cream leather headboard with his eyes closed, his head tipped to the ceiling.

I sat on the edge of the bed next to him, pushed his disheveled blond hair back, and pressed the bag to the side of his face, catching a whiff of his clean, woodsy scent in the process. I grinned inwardly and leaned closer to him for reasons unknown to me.

Maybe it was because I'd been in constant turmoil since my conversation with Evie at the coffee shop. My emotions turned more chaotic after the screaming match with my mom. I demanded she call off the party, and she used the guilt card, telling me to grow up and honor my father's dying wish. After a circular conversation that went nowhere, I had retreated to my room.

Kon opened his clear blue eyes and shifted closer to me. His eyes did a once over of my black camisole and matching polka dot sleep shorts, and I swore my skin heated. I suddenly felt off balance, and more than a little exposed.

"Why are you smiling?" he asked.

"I didn't know I was."

"Well you are. I like your smile." He shook his head like he wanted to unscramble his thoughts or take back his words, I didn't know which. "I think you hit my head harder than I realized."

"Oh, um, thanks." I choked out a nervous giggle. "So why are you here?"

Cocking his head to the side, he grabbed the frozen bag of peas from my hand and tossed them on the foot of the bed. "Don't play dumb. You blew me off tonight."

"Yeah, I'm sorry about that. Something came up."

He rubbed his temples, obviously trying to gather his thoughts before he responded. The black tattoos on his fingers stood out against the color of his skin, appearing somewhat sinister in the soft lighting.

"Did your absence have anything to do with Nico?" While his face remained a blank mask, he had a definite edge to his voice.

My muscles tensed, and I dropped my gaze to my white duvet. I wasn't ready to tell him about the party at Dominick's to announce my engagement to Nico. My mom refused to call it off before I stormed away tonight. I still held out hope she'd give in after a night of sleep.

As I weighed my words, I felt him watching me carefully, his eyes boring into me with an intensity that didn't escape my attention. It made the hairs on my arms spike as if a burst of electricity shot through my nerve endings.

I sensed he expected me to lie, which could only mean he already knew about Nico. Rather than prodding me, he remained silent, scrutinizing my every blink, twitch, and inhalation. Although he hadn't made any move to get closer to me, I felt the heat of his nearness.

I drew in an abbreviated breath and glanced to the side. Moonlight mottled the far wall, submerging the room in a silvery blue light. "You already know the answer, don't you? How'd you find out?"

"It's not a secret. I was probably the last person

to find out."

"You and me both," I mumbled.

He framed my face with his hands, forcing me to meet his stare. The warmth of his calloused fingertips made my breath hitch. "What's that supposed to mean?"

"Evie asked me about it after you left the coffee shop. That was the first time I heard anything about the party or the plan to announce our engagement." His eyes narrowed and I curled my fingers around his forearm, needing him to believe me. I didn't want to examine why I cared so much. It would be better if this whole thing exploded right now, and I let the chips fall where they may. "I can tell you don't believe me, but it's the truth."

"Are you engaged or not, Carmela? It's not a trick question." His hands skimmed down my face to the tops of my shoulders. His fingers slipped under the razor-thin strap of my camisole.

"Not really. Not officially anyway. Like I said, Nico never even proposed." Kon leaned back, and I swayed toward him a fraction of an inch like a hidden string linked us together. "Everyone expects it to happen at some point. Nico and I talked about it last week. It's what he wants. I told him I wasn't ready to commit to anything."

"So you lied when you agreed to an engagement with me to help Gian and Evie." He pursed his lips and scooted away from me. "You lied again when you agreed to work with me to find a way out of it."

"No." I tugged on his light blue tie, trying to pull him closer again. "The thing with Nico happened after I made the deal with your dad, and now...I don't know. I'm confused. I've never gone against my family and I'm scared."

I didn't know what I'd do if my family pushed me out of their lives. It happened to Nico's sister and it could happen to me. My whole world could change with a snap of Dominick's fingers. I'd lose my brother, my best friend, and my mom. I wouldn't have anything except my little online interior design business. Truthfully, I wasn't sure I could live with the fallout when I had already lost so much.

"I didn't ask you to abandon your family. You can marry Nico *after* I get him to agree to some concessions."

"Even if I go through with the engagement party, we can still make this work."

"This isn't a fucking game, Carmela. We made a deal. We had a plan. You need to stick to the script or I can't protect you. My father isn't called Bloody Alix without reason. He's not forgiving. He can be a sadistic bastard, and that's the polite way of describing him."

A shiver flitted down my spine and I wrapped my arms around my torso. "What about you? Are you forgiving? Are you my enemy? Evie said you weren't always like this. According to her, you two used to be close and you were," I cleared my throat, "her favorite person in the world. What happened?"

He cupped my chin hard enough to get my undivided attention without hurting me. His eyes were bluer than ever. The angles of his face appeared sharper and stonier than seconds earlier. His lips looked fuller and more tempting than I remembered and they were mere inches from mine.

"I don't want to talk about my sister. Ever. Not with you or anyone else for that matter. You got it? I agreed to this sham with you so she could get what she wanted. You did the same thing for your brother, and yet you won't find me questioning your relationship with him."

Guilt hit me like a punch to the gut. In a roundabout way, he helped his sister not only by breaking up her engagement with her cheating ex, but also by agreeing to explore something with me. I shouldn't judge him or his methods. It wasn't fair. God knew, I'd done plenty of things I regretted, particularly when it came to Rocco. I didn't tell him I loved him when it counted the most. In fact, I outright said I hated him and I didn't want to marry him.

"Yeah. You're right. I'm sorry. I shouldn't make any assumptions. It doesn't concern me."

His face softened and the corners of his mouth twitched. On impulse, I inched closer to him, intending to kiss his cheek. At the last moment, he moved his head and my lips brushed across his.

Sparks shot through me, and I stiffened. When I tried to put space between us, his arms circled my waist, binding me to him, denying me the separation I needed to keep my head clear.

"A genuine apology deserves a kiss. Don't you agree?" he murmured, his attention directed at my mouth.

His eyes were heavy and determined with a transparent look of a predator as though he had no intention of letting me walk away without leaving his mark. His scent enveloped me, intoxicating me, and with the speed of a bolt of lightning I went from nothing to lust and need.

His hand darted under the hem of my shirt, caressing my braless back. Goosebumps spiraled down my arms and heat pulsed low in my belly. "Let me have a taste. One taste. That's all I'm asking."

"Why?" I shot back, acutely aware of the uncharacteristic hoarseness of my voice. "Why are you doing this?"

He lifted my arms and draped them around his neck and I molded my palms over the curve of his muscles. "It's only a kiss."

My mind battled with itself. The smart thing would be to put a stop to this right now, only I couldn't. Somehow the "no" I needed to say caught in my throat, and I hovered on the knife-edge of wanting and not wanting. Every brush, tap, or circle of his fingers on my back pushed me closer to giving in.

"Do you want to complicate things even more?" My words demonstrated resistance, although my actions said the exact opposite. I tipped my head up and licked my lips in silent invitation. My nervousness was draining away second by second, only to be replaced with a needy, buzzing energy unlike like anything I'd felt before.

"I like messy, don't you?" His lips crashed against mine before I had the chance to fire off a retort, and the air separating our bodies vanished like it never existed in the first place. I found myself in his lap, my arms wrapped around his neck, and my now hard nipples squashed against the iron planes of his chest.

Our tongues tangled and I tasted wine and something uniquely him. Our ragged breaths merged into one heady moan. Our hands explored, moving freely like thieves in the night stealing what didn't belong to us. What would never belong to us.

My nerve endings fired and crackled with forbidden desire. I felt alive rather than stuck in the purgatory-like state of the last three years. Possibly longer because, quite honestly, being with Rocco never felt like this. Every touch and kiss I shared with him was gentle, caring, and respectful, as if we couldn't bear to offend one another or cross some invisible line drawn in the sand.

Tonight I didn't care about wrong or right. I already knew this was wrong, only instead of it giving me pause, it made the whole encounter combustible, dangerous, and darkly fulfilling.

With his eyes gleaming, Kon ripped my camisole over my head. The humid evening breeze from the still open balcony door wafted over my skin like a caress. Not wasting a beat, his warm mouth moved down my neck, pausing on my breasts. He took one nipple between his lips, then the other, suckling and grazing them with the blades of his teeth.

I yanked on the knot of his tie, wanting to see what was hidden beneath his shirt. He flicked my hands away, guiding me back until I sank into the mattress, my hands over my head and my heart thudding frantically inside of my chest. With a sharp tug on his blue tie, he yanked it from his neck. He dangled the shiny material from his fingertips while popping open the top two buttons of his shirt.

"I'm in control tonight," he said, knotting the tie around my wrists.

The air rushed out of my lungs and a prickle of fear raced through me. This was way out of my realm of experience. I lifted my bound arms. "I'm not sure about this, Kon."

"Then it's my job to change your mind."

Grinning wickedly, he dragged my pajama shorts down my shaky legs until they reached my ankles and tossed them on the floor. He wedged his body between my legs. His gaze fiery, his hands trailed over my dips and curves, stopping at the apex of my thighs.

He circled my entrance with his thumb. One swirl. Two swirls and then I lost count. Each time he moved deeper and deeper. Desire rushed through me so hard and fast, my hips arched off the bed, my toes curling into the threads of my sheets.

I twisted and squirmed and he steadied me with his hands. I pinched my eyes closed and turned my head into the pillow, not wanting to wake my mom on the other side of the house. Seconds later, he lowered his head, his tongue working between my legs, kissing the inside of my thighs, taunting me, teasing me. His whiskers scraped across my soft skin.

And then his tongue swiped exactly where I wanted him to be if I had the wherewithal to beg. He lapped me up, leisurely then quicker until I hovered on the brink of the best orgasm of my life. I panted, moaned, and mumbled all kinds of ridiculous things that would warm my face with humiliation in the light of the day.

I lost track of time, and all the reasons I shouldn't do this with Kon when I hadn't done this with Rocco. With Rocco every encounter was rushed, like my dad could walk in any second and put a bullet through his head. He probably would have...

Kon lifted his mouth. "Open your eyes, and I'll let you come. I don't want you thinking about anyone except me."

When his fire and ice blue eyes connected with mine, he shoved two fingers deep inside of me, curling and twisting like he knew my body better than me. He probably did. It was like he'd stolen the map to me and memorized every detail.

Shamelessly, I pushed myself against his mouth and his fingers, and he chuckled, the sound vibrating against my core and heightening my pleasure. My head whipped back and I dug my heels into his back so hard I was sure it stung, but he kept going. Licking, sucking, twisting, pumping, and there it was. An orgasm punctuated by a loud cry tore from my lungs. My limbs trembled.

Kon kept going, wringing every last ripple of pleasure from my soul. Limp with bone-deep pleasure, my body sank into the mattress, my hands still bound above my head. He slipped his tie from my wrists and draped it over my headboard.

"Did I change your mind?"

"Huh?" I mumbled, curling in a ball on my side, my eyes heavy and my mind blessedly blank. The bed shifted and Kon's weight lifted.

"Sleep, *solnyshka*," he murmured and his lips

drifted like rose petals across my forehead. "We'll talk tomorrow."

"What about the engagement party at Dominick's?"

"Find a way out of it." His words were a cutting demand, all trace of his honeyed whispers gone. "I'll get Alix to back off too."

Seconds later, I heard the balcony door close, and not too long after that, I fell asleep.

CHAPTER THIRTEEN

Konstantin

"What's the verdict?"

I spotted my father at the edge of the sidewalk, his face stern and his feet shoulder width apart. "Verdict?"

"I know you went to see Carmela two nights ago. You need to do a better job of keeping me informed."

I erased any hint from emotion from my face. My father clearly had arranged to have me followed. That was the only explanation for his statement, and he wanted me to know it. Sure, he could have a tracking device on my car or phone, except I'd parked a few blocks away and distinctly remember turning off my phone. The news pissed me the fuck off. I wouldn't let him know it, though. He liked to get under people's skin, and I'd be damned if I let him know he was dangerously close to getting under mine.

The last time I let him live rent free in my head

was when Laney went off the rails. I'd met Laney the first summer I spent in New York with my dad's family. She was literally the girl next door. Laney made the time away from the rest of my family and Nebraska bearable. In fact, she was the reason I moved to New York after high school to help my dad with his fucked up criminal enterprises.

"I told you I'd take care of this and I will."

A grin slashed his leathered face. "So you told me. I'm not sure I can trust you. You haven't been the same since the bullshit that went down with Laney."

Desperate to keep any trace of frustration off my face and out of my voice, I smirked instead. I didn't want to think about the bullshit with Laney. I trusted her, and she betrayed me first by getting hooked on drugs and then by getting pregnant.

Although she tried to pass the baby off as mine, I knew better. She'd been so far down the rabbit hole of addiction at that point that we hadn't had sex for nearly three months. While we still lived together, I'd moved her into the guest bedroom and acted more like a nursemaid than a boyfriend, holding her hand through withdrawals, trips to the hospital, and two attempted check-ins to rehab.

Sadly, I would have put up with her drug addiction, but I couldn't put up with her disloyalty. To this day, I had no clue who the father was. As far as I could tell, she didn't know either. Poor kid. Laney cleaned up during her pregnancy. Her redemption didn't last, though. In all likelihood, I'd get a call in the not too distant future informing me she was found dead with a needle in her arm.

Heroin was her drug of choice.

"I don't give a shit about Laney. I haven't thought about her in over a year."

"Speaking of Laney, she's living at her mom's house with that bastard of hers. Cute kid."

"Great. Glad to hear it."

"The boy doesn't look much like her, though. In case you had any lingering doubts, the kid's definitely not yours either. It's unusual for two blond-haired, blue-eyed parents to have a brown-eyed son."

"I never thought it was mine."

Truthfully, for one delusional week, I went along with her story, hoping the baby would be the magic bullet to solve her drug problem and our flailing relationship. That fairytale crashed and burned at the first doctor's appointment when the doctor declared Laney to be eight weeks pregnant.

Laney went crazy, first begging the doctor to check the measurements again and then calling the doctor a liar. I dragged her out of there and dropped her off at her mother's house with firm instructions to never contact me again.

"She got out of rehab a couple of weeks ago. She's clean again in case you were curious."

"I'm not, but good for her. Maybe this time it'll stick."

I didn't know what my dad's angle was. He made no secret of the fact he wanted her out of my life. I wouldn't be surprised if he had been her drug dealer at some point just to mess with us. He thought I was too young to be serious about someone I didn't know very well. Turns out he was right. The Laney I knew wouldn't have taken drugs and cheated on me, which meant I didn't know her at all.

My dad rubbed his fingers through his graying beard, his dark eyes cold and calculating. "Did you take care of Carmela?"

"You gave me a week. It's only been forty-eight hours. You'll be the first to know if and when there are any developments."

"I better be." He opened the door to the restaurant owned by the DiTonnos and waved his hand. "You first, Romeo."

"Alesio," I shook his hand. "Good to see you."

His eyes darted to my dad, then back to me. "Yeah. Likewise. Come back to my office. We need to go over a few things. But before we start, I wanted to talk to you about what happened the last time we met. I hoped we could smooth things over."

"Go ahead," I said, following him down the hall to his office.

"Renzo's a nice kid, but he hasn't been himself since his brother died in the car fire after getting into it with the Trassatos. He blames all of them for his death, including your *friend*, Carmela."

"I don't see why. His brother killed a made member of the Trassato family. Isn't that how things work in your world? An eye for an eye?"

While I didn't understand the inner workings of the Italian mafia, I knew killing a made man either resulted in death or a mob war. In the case of the Trassatos and the DiTonnos, it caused both.

The Russians weren't like the Italians. We didn't have familial or ethnic requirements. We didn't have a Don calling the shots. Our organizational structure changed constantly based on who was doing what, which was good for me. I couldn't stand all that old school shit. I needed the flexibility to act quickly, and strike while the deal was hot.

"You're right. Most people think it was justified regardless of how it happened."

"Do you think so?"

"From what I gathered, Marco and Rocco were messing around with the same woman, and she ended up pregnant. As you can imagine, neither of them liked the idea of another man dipping his dick into his territory. Passions were running high, and they both made bad decisions. As far as I'm concerned, they got what they deserved."

"That's bullshit. Rocco was engaged," I snapped, wanting to defend Carmela for some fucked up reason.

He clucked his tongue and lifted an eyebrow. "Yeah, so? What's your point? Men will be men."

"What's this got to do with us?" my dad interrupted, his tone curt.

Alesio shrugged. "I know your daughter married Gian Trassato, and I don't want you to get cold feet because you think we're still gunning for the Trassatos. The family doesn't want to get pulled into that bullshit again. I've taken care of Renzo. He won't be a problem anymore. He knows his place."

"That remains to be seen." I didn't trust that Renzo would fade quietly into the night. He was driven by revenge, and sometimes revenge left little room for logic. I'd have Anatolyi keep tabs on him and make sure he didn't cause trouble. That was all

I could do now, but if he fucked up again or interfered in my life, he'd pay dearly.

"We're businessmen first," my dad said tipping up his chin and signaling the end of the conversation. My dad was never interested in emotions and passions. According to him, they interfered with business. Money was his god to be worshiped above everything and anyone else.

"Good, seeing that I asked you here to discuss expanding our business partnership," he replied, handing both my dad and me a sheet of paper.

"What's this?" my dad asked, tossing it back on the desk.

He couldn't be bothered with the details. My dad sucked at numbers and math. Other than being his son, my talent with math was one of the main reasons he recruited me. I scored ridiculously high on every math test, and I took math classes at the local community college during high school. Numbers made sense to me. I could calculate problems in my head that took other people ten minutes to solve.

I browsed the handwritten spreadsheet, quickly double-checking the figures for the stolen car sales over the past twelve months. While the notes were purposely vague, I didn't like any of this stuff documented on paper. "Do you have a problem the payout? I did the math myself so I know it's accurate."

"It is," Alesio declared, resting his elbows on the scarred wooden desk.

I folded the paper in half and stuffed it in my back pocket. "Then why are we here?"

"I've been talking to some of my associates in the Chicago area and we'd like to replicate this business model there, with your help of course. You have the contacts to make the sales happen in Russia and our associates have officers on the pad to make any trace of our business dealings disappear. We'll set up everything. We already have a warehouse to store the cars before they're shipped."

"Ah. And who are these associates?"

"Don't worry about it. The DiTonnos are well connected in Chicago."

"We'd have to vet them personally," I countered. "I'm not going into this blind."

"I wouldn't expect you to."

My dad pulled his phone out of his pocket. "I have to take off, but it sounds like Kon has everything under control. You two can work out the details and Kon will let me know how everything shakes out."

"Right. Of course," Alesio said.

"I'll talk to you later, Dad," I chimed in, relieved he was leaving.

I couldn't stand to be in the same room as him another second. I felt like I had a black cloud hanging over my head every time I was in his company. As a kid, I looked up to him. We had inside jokes. He was interested in everything I did, always so proud of all of my accomplishments. I didn't know how or why it changed. Right around the time Laney started dabbling in drugs, he turned into a self-absorbed prick. Then I found out about the human trafficking and things went from bad to nightmare in the blink of an eye.

The door shutting pulled my head out of the trip down memory lane. "So what are the terms?"

"We want sixty percent of the profit."

I groaned inwardly. This was going to be a long fucking afternoon when I was gunning to hunt down Carmela. She'd gone radio silent again after the night in her room. While I didn't normally give a shit if I heard from a woman after spending time with her, I was far from done with Carmela and her sweet curves and sassy mouth.

CHAPTER FOURTEEN

Carmela

I plunked the binder down on Nico's desk and slouched into one of the olive green chairs opposite him. "This is everything. Let me know what you think of it."

He grinned, his deep blue eyes twinkling with amusement. My life would be so much easier if I felt something for Nico. My family approved of him. We shared a common history and life experience. Ava had told me no less than a dozen times I was crazy for being so lukewarm about him. I couldn't help it, though. My soft spot for Kon had been growing at an unsustainable pace. If it kept up at this rate, I'd be claiming something dangerously close to affection for him any day.

Flashes of him stripping off my clothes and giving me the most insane orgasm two nights ago zipped through my head. I pushed away the thoughts of Kon with the same mantra I'd been repeating since I woke up the next day wearing next to nothing.

I don't like Kon. He isn't my future. It didn't mean anything.

Nico opened the binder and flipped through a few pages. My leg bounced up and down. I stared everywhere except at his face. In all honesty, I feared his reaction. Gian loved the way I decorated his house. Nico was only the second person I knew personally to look at or consider one of my designs. The people I met through my website and communicated with via email never met me face to face.

He tapped his fingers on the arm of the tan leather desk chair, his face completely unreadable. I wanted him to like the stuff I selected for him.

Tap. Tap. Tap.

"Do you like it? Is this the sort of stuff you'd pick for yourself?"

"Me?" I asked, wondering why he wanted to know if I liked my work. I wouldn't put something together for a client if I didn't love it.

"Yes. You."

"Oh, well, it has some masculine touches that are more suitable to a bachelor than a couple, but overall it's beautiful."

"How much do you think this will cost?"

"My time or everything?"

"Everything."

"I've included high, mid, and low options for all the furniture so it depends on you. The last page has a total for each package, but you can pick and choose. The cost will be between $35,000 and $55,000."

"How much of that is for your services?"

My face had a plastic quality when I smiled at him. "I wouldn't charge you anything. We're...friends."

"Uh huh." He rubbed the back of his neck "Does that mean you aren't going to fight your family and me on the engagement?"

I blinked, then stared at him for a second. "I'm not ready to move forward yet. I heard about the engagement party in a week, and I'd like to postpone it."

"Postpone, not cancel? I can deal with that provided we set a definite date for the engagement party. Will a month be enough time to get your head wrapped around the inevitability of our marriage?"

My stomach soured. A month and my fate would be sealed. It was strange how life worked. Before Rocco died, I had my future all planned out. I'd marry him, have a couple of kids, and live happily ever after with my best friend. One stupid fight and four bullets later, and my future took a sharp turn away from a fairytale to a blank page. It had been blank for nearly three years, and now I had a month to get used to the idea of a life with Nico. A man I didn't love. A man I'd never love.

With our union, I'd have to say goodbye to Kon. A man who evoked contradictory emotions in me. A man who made me feel alive for the first time in years. A man who made me burn for him with one look or a casual brush of his hand.

A thread of sadness wove around my chest and for a beat I couldn't move. I begged my legs to snap into action and carry me away from this. Instead, numbness seeped through me, and I felt tired, defeated, and trapped. I should accept this without complaint. That was what my family expected, and I hadn't bucked their authority before because I never needed to. I had loved Rocco for most of my life, and my family loved him too. As a matter of fact, my mom admitted she and Rocco's mom started planning our wedding before we could talk. Most women related to made men weren't as lucky as me. They were told who they were going to marry and shortly after that it happened. End of story.

"I can live with that timeframe," I conceded, hoping Kon would understand and agree it was enough time to get what he needed from Nico and Dominick.

"Really?" He stood, circled the desk, and grabbed my hand, pulling me to my feet.

"Yes."

"We should go ring shopping this weekend. You can pick out anything you like. I'll make this good for you. You'll see. You won't regret marrying me."

I nodded noncommittally, wishing I believed him even for a while. Marrying him would feel like being sentenced to a gilded cage without love or companionship. I'd get every material thing a girl could ever want. I'd never get Nico, and that was fine considering I didn't want him anyway.

"What about my design proposal? Did you decide what you wanted?"

"You pick. Make sure it reflects your taste. You need to feel comfortable here. It will be your home soon enough."

"I'll keep that in mind."

My whole body itched with the urge to escape. In less than a year, I managed to arrange two marriages for myself. When I agreed to the deal with Kon, I thought I'd sold my soul to the devil. Now, however, the emptiness I felt when I looked at Nico made me wish Kon had dragged me to the altar the day after my agreement. At least with him, I felt something. Hate. Passion. Desire. Frustration. Excitement. That confusing mash of emotions relentlessly careening through me when I thought about him was better than nothing.

"I'll pick you up next Friday for dinner to celebrate our engagement. Just the two of us." He paused. "Unless you want to invite Gian and Evie."

"Um," I said, stalling for time. I had plans already, and I knew for a fact Gian didn't want to go to dinner with Nico. Sure, he'd go if I asked and he'd bring Evie with him so I could spend time with my best friend. Gian hadn't said anything to dissuade me from dating Nico, yet I got the distinct impression Gian only tolerated Nico, and he didn't want to associate with him other than on a professional level. "I can't. I have plans with Ava."

He dropped my hand and his lips thinned. "You do?"

"Yeah. Is that a problem?"

"No. I just didn't realize you two were so close."

"In the past, we weren't especially close even though we're cousins. We hung out at family things, but she contacted me when Gian and Evie got engaged. I guess she realized I was lonely."

"Well, that was nice of her," he replied looking like he wanted to say the exact opposite. Maybe Ava's flirtatious, touchy-feely behavior annoyed him more than he let on. "Do you need a ride?"

"No."

"In that case, I'll walk you out."

He opened the door and grabbed something from his pocket. "Here." He held out a gold key. "Take it. It's a key to my house. You'll need it for measurements and whatever else is necessary to get the place looking how you want it."

I took the key, stuffed it into the outside pocket of my purse, and got into the elevator with Nico. "Thanks. I guess we'll be in touch."

When the door slid open, he walked me outside and said, "Your mom invited me to Sunday dinner tomorrow, so I'll see you then."

He brushed his lips across mine. Every cell inside of me rejected the advance. At the wedding, the kiss we shared was okay. No fireworks, no desire for more. It was pleasant. Today, his touch felt like a betrayal despite the fact that Kon and I weren't anything except accomplices. I only had a month left of freedom, and I intended to use my time wisely. With any luck, I'd stumble upon my prince charming, and he'd scoop me up and take me away from the mess I made.

"Have a good week." I jogged down his front steps like the building was on fire, cursing myself and my inability to stand up to my family. Undoubtedly, I looked crazy, rubbing my hands across my lips and nearly tripping on the uneven sidewalk. When the door to Nico's building banged shut, my shoulders relaxed, and I closed my eyes to absorb everything that had happened.

"Carmela."

A hand cupped my elbow, and my eyes popped open, landing on Kon. The drawn down brim of his baseball cap didn't conceal his eyes, and they looked as cold as ice. The muscle in his lower jaw ticked like a time bomb ready to explode. His lips were firm, the skin between his brows pinched.

"Are you crazy? What are you doing here?" I hissed, unwinding his fingers one by one.

"Looking for you."

"That's stupid." My eyes darted around. "Nico would lose his mind if he saw you here."

"You kissed him."

He edged closer to me, his broad shoulders hindering my view. Without hesitating, he brushed two roughened fingers across my mouth and goose bumps spiraled down my arms. Damn him for evoking more in me with a brush of his fingers than Nico could with a press of his lips.

I studied him, trying to uncover a tiny hint of what he was thinking. I couldn't. He was like a statue, dark, impenetrable, and hard.

"You're spying on me?"

"Apparently with good reason."

I grabbed his arm and guided him down the street, stopping only when we were out of view of Nico's building. "Listen, I bought us a month. You should be happy. I followed your advice. There won't be an engagement party until sometime after that."

"So you're engaged. You're really going to

marry him?" He looked at me, wounded and a little confused. "You don't even *like* him."

"I don't see you on bended knee offering me a better deal so shut the hell up. I'll take care of my decidedly unromantic love life, and you can do whatever it is you do." I stomped my foot like a child. God, he pissed me off and made me act like an eight-year-old instead of a twenty-eight year old. "Given everything you said in the past, you should be overjoyed. I've bought you time to wrap up whatever shady thing you're working on, and you won't end up being chained to me indefinitely."

He stared at me for a second, the fire in his gaze raking down my frame, then up again. The look on his face turned my stomach upside down. I could smell the woody scent I associated with him. His eyes were like a riptide in the ocean, pulling me deeper and deeper into choppy depths the longer I looked. I swayed toward him, and the corner of one side of his mouth hooked up.

His hand landed on my hip, and he tugged me closer to him. One second he was looking at me and the next he was kissing me, all open mouth and soft tongue. A few wicked flicks of his tongue, and I forgot what we were talking about. When he finally pulled his mouth from mine, we were both out of breath.

"Come back to my house with me."

"What?" I didn't think I heard him correctly over the untamed pounding of my heart.

"Come home with me," he repeated, his voice low and gruff. His warm, minty breath floated across the side of my neck and a tingle shot down my back. Images from two nights ago banged around in my head like an invitation to sin rather than a warning.

"Why would I do that?"

"Because you want to."

"You're a little too cocky for your own good."

Butterflies exploded inside of my stomach, and I reeled them in as quickly as possible. Kon was a lot of things. He was my enemy. He was my ally. A couple of nights ago, he was my lover, but he could never be my future. I promised my father I'd consider marrying Nico. I promised Nico I would marry him in spite of knowing deep in my bones I'd never be happy.

It didn't matter, though. I was my father's daughter, a mafia princess, bred to obey my family and fulfill their wishes. As much as I willed it, an alternative future wasn't available to me. And Kon...well, we could never be anything except star-crossed lovers unless I was willing to walk away from my family, and I wasn't. They were my foundation, my life. It didn't matter anyway. Kon had told me more than once he didn't want a future with me.

"Just come back to my place for a little bit and we can talk and have a drink." He ran his hand through his already disheveled hair and a quiet self-deprecating laugh escaped his mouth. "Look, Carmela, we only have a month to get whatever this is out of our system. I can't explain it. I know you feel it too. I can tell by the way you look at me, how you respond when I touch you. The way I see it, we can either ignore this or see where this takes us. I'd prefer the latter, but it's up to you. I won't push you."

His hands skimmed the sides of my waist, barely touching the silky fabric of my dress, and like magic, my body came to life.

Crackle. Sizzle. Pop.

He pressed his lips against my neck and inhaled. They were warm, smooth, and unrelenting. My hips arched without permission, seeking more contact. More friction.

Kon was right. I did feel drawn to him. He occupied more of my thoughts than I'd ever confess out loud, and I couldn't motivate my conscience to object. My need for him debilitated my common sense. *Holy shit*, I was going to do this even knowing it was the absolute last thing I should be doing five seconds after agreeing to marry Nico.

"Okay," I whispered, tilting toward him, dizzy with his nearness. Dizzy with possibilities. Dizzy with the idea of pressing the pause button on my future and embracing the present. I wanted to be like any other woman, seeking solace in a warm body for a night without complications or expectations. "Promise me you'll drop me off at my car before midnight. I don't want my mom to worry about me."

His lips trailed up the column of my throat, and all I could think was that I had been seduced by the devil.

CHAPTER FIFTEEN

Konstantin

The entire drive to my place was a form of medieval torture. The way Carmela's nipples pebbled against the silky material of her dress tempted me to the point of distraction. More than once I forcibly trained my eyes on the road in front of me so we didn't end up wrapped around a stop sign and kill a half-dozen pedestrians in the process. Then the way she licked her lips like she wanted to tackle me and have her way with me. Fuck, I couldn't go there.

The ride on the elevator was another exercise in control. I studied the lit panel, counting the floors in my head instead of glancing at her because one glimpse was all it would take for me to rip her little dress over her head. While elevator sex may sound enticing on any other day, I thought it might send her running in the opposite direction.

The minute we crossed the threshold of my apartment, all bets were off. I flipped the lock and flattened Carmela against the door. Her breath rushed out of her lungs and the picture on the wall rattled. The steady beep of my alarm chimed. Punching in the code with one hand, I pinned her arms above her head with the other, taking my time to drink in the sight in front of me.

Her pupils nearly eclipsed her golden irises. Her chest rose and fell like she'd run up the ten flights of stairs instead of taking the elevator. Her nearly black hair curled around her shoulders, and the kicker was, she had no clue how sexy she was.

My mouth crashed against hers, our tongues lashing like weapons. The possessive side of me I didn't know existed until I saw Nico kiss her raged with the need to wipe any trace of him away. My blood roared through my ears, and all I could think about was ripping Nico's lips from his smug face.

Gasping, she broke our connection, her fingernails clawing into the tops of my shoulders. My lips traced the graceful arch of her neck, biting her right beneath her ear and sucking on the smooth skin until I left a mark.

I curved my splayed hands around her round backside, and one of her bare legs curled around me, which was a green light in my mind, one I didn't intend to let go to waste. My hands skimmed up her body, taking her sexy little dress on the journey with me.

I palmed her between her legs, rubbing in a circular pattern and getting drunk and hard as fuck with every moan and roll of her hips. On instinct, my other hand circled the front of her throat, forcing her to look at me and only me. Not breaking eye contact with her, I slid her white lace panties to the side, hunting for the lips of her pussy. The second I found her slick entrance I drove two fingers inside, anchoring my thumb on her clit.

I moved slowly at first, watching her face twist with a combination and pleasure and pain.

"Kon, oh hell, like that. Exactly like that," she mumbled, her words slurred and thick with lust.

I slammed my lips against hers, my finger picking up speed and curving with the exact angle to bring her to a fever pitch. She tugged at my pants until she had them over my hips. As much as I wanted to drag this out, I couldn't. I'd wanted to slide inside her for too many months to wait another second.

When I pulled out my fingers, her eyes went wide. I ripped her panties from her body and her lips tipped up. *Damn, this woman.* She was naughty and nice wrapped up in one helluva sultry package.

I tilted up her hips, and in a single thrust, I was inside of her. She was tight, yet wet enough that I didn't meet much resistance. Her walls squeezed around me and all I could think was this woman was made for me. A lengthy moan echoed through my apartment, and I couldn't be sure if it came from her or me. Maybe both of us.

She circled her legs around my waist, and her hips started undulating. I couldn't go slow or attempt to be gentle. My dick hammered in and out of her. Flesh slapped against flesh. The picture banged against the wall repeatedly, only stopping when it fell to the floor and the glass shattered around our feet.

I pulled one lace covered nipple into my mouth, then the other. Her hips moved faster, matching my punishing pace.

Her eyes fluttered shut. Sweat curved down my spine. My shirt clung to my skin. Her fingers dug into my biceps.

"Oh God, Kon. I'm..."

My teeth graze her ear, and I groaned. "I know, *solnyshka,* I know." And I did know. I could feel her hot, wet pussy gripping me in waves. I kept pumping, my fingers digging into her thighs.

Her sex drunk eyes popped open and she licked her bottom lip. I couldn't hold back for another second. I exploded, releasing my lust for this woman that had been building for years.

Burying my head into the crook of her neck, I inhaled her familiar lemon scent now mixed with the smell of sex. It had to be the best smell in the world.

Her legs slid to the floor, and it felt as if New York City had conspired against us, deciding to go completely silent. No cars honked, the elevator didn't ding, the air conditioning unit didn't kick on, my crazy neighbor didn't crank up his TV. Enough time passed that the sweat cooled on my skin.

I opened my mouth to break the awkward silence hanging over us like an invisible shroud. Before I could get any words out, she forced me away from her, glass from the now broken picture crunching under the soles of my boots.

"I need to go home," she whispered, her voice shaky and unsure. She reached for her dress, aborting the action when she saw the glass from the picture sprinkled over the soft material. What a fucking mess. She couldn't wear it home.

I scrutinized her for any hints of her state of mind. I didn't see anything except a slight tremor in her hands, which could be good or bad. "Stay. We'll have dinner."

She swallowed hard. "Where's the bathroom? I need to put myself together."

"Down the hall on the right. There's a robe on the back of the door if you want to…" This didn't need to be so uncomfortable. We enjoyed the hell out of each other. We were both willing participants. I liked her more than any other woman that had flitted through my life lately, and I think she felt the same. Unfortunately, I had no idea how to ease the sudden tension.

Nodding a little too vigorously, she skirted around the shattered picture, her dress, and me.

Seconds later, the bathroom door slammed and I heard the distinct sound of crying.

Fuck.

This was the reason I stayed clear of anything resembling a relationship since Laney. I couldn't stand the tears, the fighting, and the constant yo-yoing of emotions.

I fastened my pants and made my way down the hall, knowing in all likelihood, she didn't want to talk to me.

"Hey." I cracked open the door and leaned my shoulder into the doorjamb. "Is everything okay?"

Clearly, she wasn't. I didn't know why I asked such an asinine question. She sat on the edge of the tub deck clothed in my too big robe with her face in her hands and her shoulders shaking.

"Can you leave me alone?" she mumbled through her fingers, her sobs intensifying with each syllable out of her mouth.

I knelt in front of her and peeled her hands from her face. Mascara streaked her cheeks. Her eyes were swollen and her skin was splotchy. "You're all right, Carmela. Just breathe, and talk to me about what's going on in that head of yours."

"No, I'm really not." Her legs bounced up and down. "And it doesn't matter. I'm not your problem. Just give me something to wear and I'll get out of your way and cry somewhere else."

"Tell me what's wrong."

"I hate you. I hate that I did that with you. I hate that I feel anything for you. I hate that my family is pushing me to marry Nico. I hate, well, everything."

My lips twitched. "That's a lot of hate."

"Ugh." She punched me in the shoulder. "Why are you smiling? You're so annoying. Have you always been a pain in the ass?"

"According to Evie…yes."

"You probably tortured her when you were kids."

"There was that one time when I gave her favorite doll to the dog as a chew toy. If you tell her I admitted it, though, I will deny it."

She barked out a laugh and my lungs tightened. Damn, I liked making this girl laugh.

"You forgot who you're talking to. I'm a Trassato. I probably got the confession on tape and I'm going to use it against you as leverage."

I ran my hand down her cheek to her jaw, erasing

131

the last evidence of her tears. "Is that right?"

"You'll have to wait and see."

"So are you going to tell me why you were crying?"

"I don't want to. You'll think it's trivial."

"Try me."

"Ugh. Fine." Her eyes flickered up and down like she couldn't stand to look at me. I didn't like it. I wanted all of her attention. "I've only done *that* with Rocco, and not very often either. Okay? Now go ahead and make fun of me."

"What do you mean?" I asked, though I had a damn good idea what she meant. For reasons I refused to examine, I wanted her to clarify. "You and Rocco dated for a long time."

"Yeah, well, we never spent much time alone once we hit puberty, and my parents made it known that we shouldn't go *there*. Once we got engaged, we snuck around a few times, but Rocco gave me this whole speech about not wanting to disappoint our parents and having our whole life in front of us."

For several seconds, I didn't say a single thing until I couldn't hold it in any longer. I burst out laughing.

"You jerk!" She smacked me on the side of my head. "I can't believe you're laughing at me right now. I told you something extremely personal and private, and you think it's a joke?"

"No, *solnyshka,* I'm not laughing at you. I'm laughing at Rocco."

"Huh?" She blinked a few times. "What do you mean?"

"Let's just say, if you were my girlfriend, my fiancée, or my whatever, I wouldn't let anything stop me from kissing you. Touching you. In fact, I'd spend a considerable amount of my waking hours plotting to get you in my bed."

A million dollar smile spread across her face, and my heart stopped momentarily. She was insanely beautiful. "Really?"

"Really. Now tell me what you want for dinner. I'm starving."

CHAPTER SIXTEEN

Carmela

When I woke up at Kon's place this morning, my phone was dead. Without question, my mom was coming out of her skin with worry, and in all likelihood, she had called Gian. This knowledge didn't compel me to run home and fall into line with a pile of apologies on my lips. It actually motivated me to embrace my freedom and linger in bed with Kon, taking pleasure in my first sleepover with a man. Taking pleasure in the momentary disconnect from the expectations of my family.

By the time I pulled into the garage of my childhood home, I'd been gone for over thirty hours. My stomach dropped along with all hope no one noticed my absence when I passed Gian's black SUV in the driveway.

Deciding to face the firing squad, I went into the house rather than using the stairway to the apartment over the garage. It would be futile to hide. The confrontation would happen either way, but if I met it head on, it gave me more power...or at least that was what I told myself as my sneakers squeaked over the marble tiled floor. Thankfully I'd had the forethought to change into my gym clothes in the trunk of my car before I drove home.

"Where have you been?" my brother said the minute I entered the great room. The familiar tang of garlic and tomato sauce hit my nose.

Sunday dinner. Crap.

I paused for a beat, taking in the scene in front of me. My brother stood in front of the fireplace with an elbow on top of the old world precast fireplace mantle. Evie sat on one of the gray armchairs, picking at the hem of her shirt. My mom was curled up on the cream colored sectional with her head in her hands. I didn't see Nico anywhere, which was a good thing. My mom must have covered for me.

"I went out with a friend," I replied, tossing my purse onto the glass coffee table and dropping onto the arm of the sofa. "What is everyone doing here?"

"Dammit, Carmela." Gian slapped his hand against the top of the mantle. "You know exactly why we're here. You didn't come home last night. You didn't answer your phone. No one had any idea where to find you. Nico said you left his place around three yesterday. That was over twenty-four hours ago."

"So what? I'm twenty-eight, not sixteen. I don't need to tell you guys where I am every second of the day."

"*Madon!*" My mom jumped to her feet, a red blush staining her cheeks. "When you still live under my roof, you are accountable to me. That means taking the time to give me a courtesy call or text to let me know you won't be home. I don't think that's too much to ask, do you?"

"No. I forgot, and my phone ran out of charge. I'm sorry, Mama, but you didn't need to worry. I'm a big girl. I lived on my own for three years before Dad died."

"What are you talking about? You need me. I feed you, I clothe you, I give you a place to live. And all I ask in return is for you check in with me so I'm not up all night worrying about you." A tear trickled down her face, and she might as well have stabbed me in the chest. "I lost my husband not too long ago. I can't take this, Carmela. I feel like I aged five years last night. I kept picturing you dead or injured in some alley somewhere."

"I'm sorry I upset you," I mumbled, shame and frustration bottling up in my chest. I hadn't set out to hurt her or my family, and I didn't do anything thousands of other twenty-eight year olds did every day. "You're probably right. It's time for me to get my own place again. This was only meant to be a temporary move."

My brother crossed the room and stood only a foot from me. "How are you going to do that? You don't have a job, you don't have any income except what comes from the family."

"I have money. I do design jobs on the side."

"Oh, I know all about your design jobs, and they won't keep you afloat. Not in New York."

"Are you threatening to cut me off?"

He cocked his head to the side. "You tell me, Carmela. *Should* I cut you off?"

"What the hell's that supposed to mean?"

Evie jumped up. "Guys, stop it. Don't fight. You're upsetting your mom more. Carmela made a mistake. It's not a big deal. She came home in one piece. That's all that matters. Cut her some slack."

"Evie, take my mom for a walk. I want to talk to my sister alone. We have a few things to discuss."

Sighing, Evie stood, and grabbed my mom's hand. "Show me the flowers the gardener planted yesterday." She paused at the glass patio door and glanced over her shoulder. "Gian, remember that Carmela gave us space when we got engaged. She supported us. We need to do the same for her."

"Yeah, yeah. Get out of here, Evie. Have a little faith in me. I'm not going to be a jerk."

The door thudded closed, and Gian sighed heavily. "Tell me what's going on with you and Konstantin Trincher."

I wanted to deny everything. My brother had lied to me about his engagement with Evie. I didn't owe him the truth, but his hands sliced through the air, stopping me in my tracks.

"You can stop right there, Carmela. I want the truth. I can't protect you from the fallout if you keep me the dark."

"The fallout. What fallout?"

"Mom called Nico first thing this morning when you didn't come home last night. We had to call him back later this afternoon and tell him you were sick and not to come over tonight."

"So? Nico doesn't own me. I can do what I want without his permission."

"You're his fiancée. What's he supposed to think

when you disappear overnight?"

"That I was busy. That I have a life. That I have friends. Honestly, I don't care. Nico and I aren't like you and Evie. He doesn't love me, and I don't love him."

"You're sadly mistaken, Carmela. He won't overlook what happened last night. Even if he truly doesn't care, no man wants to look like a fool."

"I don't know what you're talking about."

"Don't play games with me. I know you spent the night with Konstantin Trincher, and if I know it, you can bet your ass Nico knows it too."

I stopped breathing for a second, my mind racing in time with my blood pressure. "How did you find out? Do you have people watching me?"

"Of course I do. You're my sister. After everything that our family's been through in the past couple of years, I won't let anything happen to you. I can't. It'd kill me." He steepled his fingers together in front of his mouth, his eyes distant. "I promised Dad I'd make sure you were taken care of and happy. That's all I want. That's all Mom wants too."

"I know. I'm sorry if my decisions hurt you guys. I love all of you, you know that. I can't make choices solely to make my family happy, though, and right now that's what it feels like. I know everyone expects me to marry Nico, and I'm scared to death that it will be a terrible mistake."

For a beat, panic spread across Gian's face, his eyes wild, his mouth ajar. He shook his head. "Konstantin will destroy you. You realize that, don't you? Nico may not be the love of your li—"

"He's not. Rocco was. That will never change. Anyone who comes after him is a cheap imitation." My voice was a little unhinged. Hell, I *felt* a little unhinged.

Last night with Konstantin had me a little off balance in more ways than one, and that was before I walked into something that resembled a family intervention. Sex had never been like that with Rocco. Being intimate with him was like slipping into an old, favorite pair of jeans. Everything was familiar. Sweet even.

In contrast, last night with Kon was explosive, passionate, and greedy. He felt incredible. He tasted wonderful. He smelled…perfect. That was why I needed to reel myself in before I confused sex for love.

"Sweetie." Gian placed his hands on my shoulders, a look of pity on his face. "You shouldn't keep Rocco on a pedestal. He wasn't perfect. He did dumb shit, made bad decisions. He'd still be alive if he had walked away from that fight with the DiTonno kid. He had no business being there that night. Too many people died because of his choices."

I slumped back into the couch, feeling frustrated and foolish. "What did he do?"

"Let the dead be dead, and forgive their trespasses. There is no point in dredging up history. It's a waste of time and energy."

"Was Rocco cheating on me before he died?"

"We're not having this conversation."

"Just tell me. I need to know. We fought that night, and I can't stop feeling guilty about the things

I said to him. Maybe if I knew he wasn't innocent I could get closure."

"Honestly, Carmela, I don't know. Where'd all this come from? Did Nico say something?"

"No." I chewed on the corner of my lower lip, plotting my response. "I overhead someone saying one of the DiTonnos killed Rocco over a woman."

Gian glanced to the side, his eyes glinting with something. Anger? Sympathy? When he faced me again, he had scrubbed all traces of emotion. "Marco?"

"I guess. I didn't catch his name."

"Shit, I won't lie to you. You deserve truth so here it is. Before he died, there were rumors. I confronted Rocco and he denied it. He had excuses and alibis, and most of them made sense."

Dread settled deep inside of me and cotton gathered in my mouth, my self-preservation begging me to halt the line of questioning. "Did you believe him?"

"I knew him my whole life, and I gave him the benefit of the doubt. Maybe I shouldn't have. He might not have died if I had pushed harder."

The words left a gaping chasm in the heart I thought I no longer had. It was as close to an admission as I'd ever get, yet it didn't give me comfort or closure. Not even close. On the contrary, it made me feel worse than before, and I was sick and tired of feeling shitty about everything in my life.

"You think he was cheating on me." My voice shattered on the last word and with it came the urge to cry. I swallowed, but it did nothing to stop the

140

inevitable. Pain, sorrow, and regret inched up my throat. A whimper echoed through the room.

Oh God. Not again.

Between my dad and Rocco, I thought I had shed all the tears allotted to me in this lifetime. Apparently, I was wrong. The possibility that my relationship with Rocco was one-sided made me want to take a scalpel to my chest and carve out the shattered pieces of my heart along with every memory of us together.

"Carmela, come here." Gian pulled my cold and trembling body into his arms, holding me close for a few beats before releasing me. My vision was fuzzy around the edges and my stomach swirled with nausea. I had to be in shock. "Don't do this to yourself. Rocco loved you, don't ever doubt that. And there's nothing you can do to change the past. Rocco and Marco are dead, so we'll probably never know the truth. Let it go. Let Rocco go. Please."

He was right. It was easier said than done, though. Grimacing, I swatted away the salty tears burning my cheeks. "So I can marry Nico and live happily ever after?"

He grasped my chin with enough force to get my attention. "I thought you liked Nico. I thought you wanted to marry him."

"Oh please, you're my brother. Don't you know me at all?"

He frowned. "What do you mean?"

"When we're together, I don't feel anything for him. Just a lot of nothing. Maybe I'm getting cold feet about the whole thing and looking for reasons not to marry him. I mean…you and Mom like him, right? And Dad trusted him or he wouldn't have put the whole thing in motion. Maybe I'm too fucked up to see a good thing even when it's in front of my face."

"Nico and I don't always see eye to eye. He pissed me the fuck off before Evie and I got married. Lately he's backed off, though, which probably has more to do with you than me."

"That's not exactly comforting."

He squeezed my upper arms. "You don't have to marry him. We can find a way out of this. I want you to be happy. You deserve to be happy after everything that's happened to you."

"But Mom—"

"Will get over it. Sure, she'll be embarrassed and she might yell at you. Her anger will pass. You know how she is."

"What do you think I should do?"

"I won't force you down the aisle. Follow your heart."

I nodded, staring absently at the family picture above the fireplace. I guess in a small way I was lucky my dad wasn't around. He would force me to marry Nico without batting an eye. He was more old school than Gian. Be that as it may, Gian's support might not help me.

"Doesn't matter what you do if Uncle Dominick decides otherwise."

His expression darkened, and his jaw tensed. "Yeah, but you have a better shot of changing his mind if I'm on your side. I'm sure we can come up with some dirt on Nico to make Dominick think twice."

"Maybe. We can figure it out later. I'm starving." I smiled, signaling the end of our conversation. "Did you guys already eat dinner?"

"No. We were waiting for you."

"In that case, I'll go find Mom and Evie, and let them know it's safe to come back inside."

When I pivoted to leave, he grabbed my hand. "I want to clarify one thing. I'll support your decision to break things off with Nico, but all bets are off if I find out you're hanging out with Konstantin Trincher."

"What are you saying?"

"I want you to cut all ties with him. He hurt Evie. I won't let him hurt you too when we both know things with him won't end well. Can you do that?"

Apart from stiffening, I didn't react. "It won't be a problem," I agreed, my voice thin like a frayed rope.

It was a flat out lie. I had no intention of kicking Kon out of my life. Last night's attempt to get him out of my system had categorically failed. Only an hour had passed since I left his place, and I already missed him. Missed his touch, missed his cocky grin. It was too early in our non-relationship to miss him, which said a lot about how deep my feelings for him already ran. Honestly, I couldn't remember feeling so much for anyone after such a short period.

CHAPTER SEVENTEEN

Konstantin

"Carmela," I whispered when she crossed the threshold of her bedroom. I'd been waiting here for over an hour. Dumbest fucking move I'd ever made considering Gian's car was sitting in the driveway when I scaled the wall.

Her hand flew to her chest, and she stumbled back into the door. I turned on the television to mute our voices if her mom wandered down the hall.

"I didn't mean to scare you."

She looked up at me, the flickering television highlighting one side of her face and the darkness of the room shadowing the other. "My brother and Evie are downstairs."

"I watched them pull out of the driveway thirty seconds ago."

"Why are you here?"

I didn't know why I was here. No, that was a lie. My plan to fuck away my need for this woman last night backfired big time, making me crave her more than before I touched her. On some level, last night was the worst decision I'd ever made, and I'd made a lot of bad decisions in my life. However, that didn't stop me from crawling back for more tonight.

"I wanted to make sure you're okay."

"What do you mean?"

"Lock the door so we can talk."

"It's been a crazy night." She blew out an audible stream of air, and her shoulders hunched over. "Can't we table this conversation until tomorrow?"

"*Jesus*, do you have to be so argumentative? Lock the fucking door."

"This is a really bad idea." Her hand fumbled behind her back. "No one found out about you being here the other night, but they're suspicious now. They'll be watching more closely."

When the lock clicked, I said, "I knew they'd be waiting for you, and I didn't want anything to happen to you."

"They wouldn't hurt me."

"What about Gian?" I worried about my sister being with a hard ass like Gian. Even supposing he wasn't a sadistic son of a bitch like my father or Nico DeAngelo, my sister was soft and artsy. She loved acting and dancing, and she lived her life with her head stuck in the clouds. Gian ruled the men under him with an iron fist. I'd slit his throat if he broke Evie's spirit.

Carmela studied me for a moment, her teeth worrying her lower lip. "Gian's protective of the people he loves, including your sister. You don't have to worry about him with her, you know. He would never hurt her or me. You've never come right out and asked about him, but I think you might be curious. You miss her, don't you?"

Her proclamation hung in the air, baiting me. I refused to bite. I couldn't talk about my sister with her. Evie's absence in my life felt too raw. The state of our relationship made a mockery out of all of the days we spent catching up after I got home from New York every summer. We'd get lost in the cornfields neighboring our property, eating raw corn until our stomachs ached, and making promises to always be close. It didn't look like that was in the cards anymore.

"What'd they say?" I asked, changing the subject, hating the choppiness in my voice.

"Nothing important. They're worried about me."

"That's it?"

She padded across the patterned carpet floor and sprawled out on her bed. She closed her eyes, leaving a soft, relaxed look on her face. "I don't want to talk about it. I'm exhausted. I don't think we got more than three hours of sleep last night. You should go home. You have to be exhausted too."

"They want you to stay away from me." It wasn't a question.

"Yeah." Her eyelids cracked open. "My brother has someone tailing me, so he knows we've been meeting up. Obviously, he doesn't approve. He said he'd support my decision not to marry Nico if I stayed away from you."

"I'm not surprised he's keeping tabs on you," I

answered. I couldn't blame Gian for wanting her to stay away from me. It showed he cared about her. I respected that.

"What are we going to do?"

I crossed the room, removed her shoes, and rubbed the arches of each foot. "We're going to go to bed. Get some rest, and we'll figure out a plan later."

"Yeah?"

"Yeah."

She propped herself up on her elbows, and her dark wavy hair looked like an inky waterfall next to the moonlit white duvet. "Don't you think that's risky?"

"I don't care." I shimmied her fitted black pants down her legs, and she pulled her shirt over her head and unclasped her bra. A pang shot through me as I took in the image in front of me. Her golden eyes glowed in the dim light. Her nipples were dark pink and hard, her skin like silk. Her curves made my mouth water and my dick come to attention. I never understood how Laney could crave drugs enough to ruin her life. Looking at Carmela, I finally identified with the freedom in losing control because I was damn close to jumping into the abyss with her. Nothing good would come of my growing attachment, and despite knowing this deep in the recesses of my soul, I couldn't stop myself from reaching for her time and time again.

I tossed my keys and wallet on her dresser and climbed on the bed. I hovered above her, trying to decide what I wanted to do first. There were so many options. So many things left to explore. So many things to check off my list before I had to hand her over to that asshole Nico forever.

Holding her jaw in one hand, I pressed my mouth against hers. Her tongue dove through my lips, swirling, tasting, and setting my cock on fire.

"What about your clothes?" she asked, her lips still against mine, her voice breathy, and her body vibrating with unconcealed desire.

I came to my knees and grabbed the hem of my t-shirt, yanking it over my head. I unbuckled my pants and pushed them down my hips. I could get used to having this woman next to me every night.

I lowered my body to hers, barely holding back a groan when my skin met hers. "I think I like you more than I should."

"No, you only like screwing me. That's what you told me last night."

"Hmm, I don't know what you're talking about. I would never say anything like that."

A knock thudded against her door. Her eyes flared. Her chest rose and fell rapidly against the pads of my fingers.

"Oh shit," she whispered.

"Carmela, can I talk to you for a second?" Evie's distinct voice floated through the room.

My muscles tautened, ready to flee. Oh shit was right. I had no interest in facing off with Gian or my sister tonight or anytime in the near future.

"I thought you said they left," she murmured next to my ear.

"They did."

The door handle rattled, and I jumped off the bed, snagging my t-shirt and pants from the bed.

"One second. I'm changing." Carmela rushed across the room, flung open her bathroom door, and pulled on a short silver robe, knotting it at her waist.

"Oh, okay," Evie said.

Carmela pointed at the bathroom, and mouthed, "Hide in here."

CHAPTER EIGHTEEN

Carmela

I cracked open my door, smoothing a hand over my chest, trying to stop my heart from jumping out of my chest and plopping onto the floor near my feet. "Hi. I thought I saw you guys leave."

"We did. Gian forgot the leftovers, and you know how much he misses your mom's cooking."

Evie couldn't cook to save her life. Her culinary skills started and ended with canned soup and raw vegetables. If my brother wanted a real Italian meal, he had to call my mom or do it himself. He didn't seem to mind, though. As far as I could tell, he believed the world revolved around Evie, and that was exactly the way it should be. Quite honestly, I'd give my left arm to have a man look at me the way Gian looked at her.

"That explains everything."

Chuckling, she waved her hand toward my room. "Can I come in?"

"Ah…" I glanced over my shoulder, checking on

the closed bathroom door.

"Just for a second. I'm sure you're drained, and Gian can't stay long anyway. He has a meeting early in the morning."

"Sure." I flipped on the light and sat on the edge of my now messy bed, discreetly smoothing out the wrinkles with hand.

She followed me in and leaned on the edge of my dresser. "We didn't get a chance to talk tonight."

"No. Not really."

"I hope Gian didn't give you a hard time when your mom and I went outside."

"We worked it out."

"Yeah, Gian said you'd stay away from Kon, and he'd help you with the Nico situation."

"He told you?"

She shrugged, sheepishly. "We don't keep many secrets from each other, and he knows I'm worried about you. I don't like this whole thing you have going with my brother. I don't trust him. He's not right for you."

She swept her hand along the top of my dresser, pausing when she spotted Kon's keys. Frowning, she scooped them up and studied the icon dangling from the chain, her mouth pressed into a firm disapproving line.

The possibility of being caught with Kon in my room made my stomach plummet like I'd swallowed a leaden balloon. If she summoned Gian, this night would end in a fistfight or worse.

At twenty-eight years old, I should be able to do what I wanted with whom I wanted. Unfortunately, my family didn't work that way, which was both a good and bad thing. Without a doubt, I loved them, and I would never dream of doing anything to hurt or disappoint them intentionally, but I'd be the first to admit their love was stifling. They monopolized every weekend, weeknight, and holiday with birthday parties, baptisms, weddings, and the plain old Sunday dinner just to name a few, which didn't leave much time for anything else.

"Is something wrong?" I said when she remained stubbornly silent.

Her mouth opened, closed, and then she dumped the keys back on the dresser right next to Kon's wallet. They hit the wood surface with a loud clunk. She stared at me for a second, her face pale. The faint laughter from the television did little to alleviate the awkward silence.

"I-I have to go. I can't be part of this. I won't."

I shot up from my bed, hooking my hand around her wrist right as she neared my door. "Don't say anything," I whispered not wanting anyone, including Kon, to overhear me.

"I can't lie to Gian. He'd never forgive me. We don't keep secrets," she hissed.

"I'm not asking you to lie to your husband."

"Then what?"

"If Gian comes in here, things will get ugly. You don't want that, and neither do I. You may think you hate your brother, but I know you, Evie. You don't want anything bad to happen to Kon, and that's precisely what will happen if you tell Gian."

Her hand drummed against her thigh. Time froze. I couldn't get enough air into my lungs as I waited. Right now, she was my judge, jury, and executioner.

"Okay. Okay," she finally conceded. "You're probably right. I'll cover for you this time, and that's it. Don't ask me again."

"I won't."

She scanned the corners of my room. "Get him the hell out of here and tell him not to come back. I don't want him in my life or yours. He's toxic. My whole family is toxic. They'll drag you through Hell before they're done with you."

I should have called her out. After all, this was my home and my life. I didn't, though. I took her moment of reprieve and embraced it. "Thanks, Evie."

The second she left, I closed and locked the door behind her, and slid down the wall, tears rolling down my cheeks. I'd made such a mess of my life. I didn't want to marry Nico. I'd been lying to myself, thinking I could merge my life with someone who I didn't want. Who I didn't love. And Kon...well, I couldn't give him up. The thought of kicking him out of my life made my insides twist. Somehow he'd come to represent my freedom and a rebellion from what everyone expected of me, and I wasn't ready to clip back on the Trassato family leash. The worst part was that I liked Kon. More than liked him.

Kon crouched down in front of me and his hands circled my waist. "Hey, is everything okay?"

"Evie knows you were in here."

He tipped up my chin, his brow furrowing when he spotted my stupid tears.

"I know. I heard."

"She saw your keys and wallet on my dresser. She's not going to say anything."

"I'm sorry I forgot about them. Are you okay?"

"Yes. You should probably go, though. I'm sure she'll act weird the entire way home and Gian will weasel the information out of her. We probably only have a half hour grace period here."

"I'm not leaving." His lips brushed over mine, and he unknotted my robe.

"Gian—"

"Fuck Gian." He wrapped my legs around his waist and carried me to the bed, pausing near the edge. "I only care about you and right now you need me. I need you."

"If he comes back—"

He placed a finger against my lips. "We'll deal with it."

He set me on the bed, pushed the robe off my shoulders, and I shivered when the cool air hit my breasts. His eyes burning like blue flames and the light from the television highlighting the sharp angles of his face, he unbuckled his pants. They, along with his boxer briefs, fell to the floor with the clunk of his belt.

In two strides he nudged his hips between my dangling legs. Reaching up, I sifted through the silky strands of his blond hair. A devastatingly sexy smirk split his face and his mouth sealed against mine. Rocco's kisses made me glow with happiness, yet they didn't compare to Kon's. No one kissed like him. His taste was as intoxicating as the grappa my uncle served after Christmas dinner.

He seduced me with every brush of his lips and curl of his tongue.

His tattooed hand blanketed my breast, his calloused thumb rubbing over my stiff nipple. I tugged at the roots of his hair, pulling him on top of me, fusing our bodies together, desperate to have more.

The minute his bare chest collided with mine, a shiver zipped down my spine, and I whimpered in relief. His erection slid against me until I was dazed, needy, and oh so greedy. A sweet ache burrowed beneath my chest. We had sex so many times last night I'd lost count, and now I realized I'd never get enough of the way he made me feel.

Of course, somewhere buried deep in my brain and quilted with a dreamlike haze, I wondered if Evie was right and Kon was toxic. A toxic addiction that would destroy me some time not too far in the future. Only unlike Rocco and my father's death, Kon could deal the final defining blow, one impossible to recover from.

I was a Trassato. He was a Trincher. I should keep my guard raised in anticipation of treachery. In the beginning, we were enemies united in the common goal in finding a path out of the deal we made. Now we were something else, something fuzzy, indistinct, and undefined. More than that, he'd never indicated his intentions toward me had changed. As far as I knew, he still didn't want to marry me, and on the outside chance he did, it would never happen.

All thoughts of why I should stop this fizzled the second his mouth slid down my jaw to my neck, to the swells of my breasts, moving lower and lower. Fire licked at my skin. With his lips, tongue and fingers, he worshiped me, taking his time, and cataloging my responses like he had all of eternity to use the information, and not only tonight.

"Kon," I gasped wanting nothing more than to have him inside of me.

"What do you want, *solnyshka*?"

"You, inside me."

He chuckled against my lower belly, and the gruff sound sent a blast of lust directly to my core. "I'm getting there. I want to taste you first."

I mumbled indistinguishably in response because I wanted that too. He centered himself between my thighs, his knees dropping to the floor. Bracing my upper body on my elbows, I watched him lick my clit and moaned.

"See? You needed this."

His tongue swirled, plunged in and out, gravelly and silky at the same time. Too soon, full body trembles rippled through me, signaling both how far and how close I was to falling over the edge. My hips arched. My toes curled. My fingers clawed at the bedding while I begged and pleaded for him to let me come.

He didn't give in. He climbed on top of me and settled his thick cock at the apex of my thighs, his heavy-lidded stare boring into me.

"Now you can come," he said, thrusting inside me, filling me with unparalleled perfection. I screamed his name, wondering why I had begged for more of his tongue because this was so much better. One pump of his hips and I was there, falling, spiraling to the point of no return. My sex pulsed around him, greedily pulling him in and refusing to let go, and he was right there with me, our breaths in sync, our movements the perfect counterpart.

With an exaggerated groan, he pumped into me again and again. The bed squeaked, the bottle of water fell off my nightstand, and he pushed me higher and higher.

My body shuddered. My lips were numb. Nothing except that moment and the way I felt as we melded into one mattered. When he stopped moving, I closed my eyes and my legs flopped to the side, the turmoil of this night forgotten, the adrenaline and endorphins gradually retreating.

"We aren't even close to being finished," he rumbled next to my ear. Chills cascaded down my arms.

"Really?" I replied without opening my eyes. I would do anything he wanted if it entailed him making me feel this good. "What do you have in mind?"

The bed dipped, and one way or another he managed to scoop me up and stand with my legs circling his hips, him still buried inside of me like he couldn't bear to be separated. I knew I couldn't. I tucked my face into the spot where his neck met his shoulder, inhaling his scent that had become achingly familiar over the past couple of weeks and something that would be burned into my memory forever. Moments like this made me believe nothing could go wrong.

"All good things."

Thirty seconds later, he turned on my rain showerhead, and we stepped inside.

***

Sometime before the sky lightened, I woke to the husky rumble of Kon's voice.

"I need to go. I'll call you later."

I stretched my arms over my head, rolled to my side, and pulled the sheet over my still naked body. He brushed his lips over mine.

"Don't leave. We still have a couple of hours before my mom gets up."

He trailed his hand along my arm. "I'd love to stay and make you breakfast, but we've already pushed this too far. I need to go."

"When will I see you again?"

I shouldn't have asked him this. Common sense told me I needed to file away the memory of last night and forget about him like I promised Gian. I couldn't do it, because for the first time in over three years, I felt as if I had a reason to get up in the morning and live my life without a cloud over my head.

He hesitated with his hand on the handle of the balcony door. "Your family isn't going to like it. Gian will be watching you now more than ever."

"I know. We still haven't figured what to do about the arrangement we made with your dad, and I'm kind of getting used to having you around."

He grinned and cracked open the door. "Do you have a soft spot for me, Carmela Trassato? And here I thought you'd hate me forever."

I grabbed the pillow off my bed and tossed it at him. He easily batted it away. "Ugh. Don't be a jerk."

His deep chuckle followed him out the door.

CHAPTER NINETEEN

Konstantin

"Hooray! You made it," Carmela said, beaming.

She stood in front of the commercial range, her curvy body drowning in a white chef's jacket, her glossy hair slicked back in a low ponytail, a shiny spatula in her hand.

"You didn't think I'd blow off a home cooked meal, did you?"

"I sent you through quite the obstacle course to get here. Sorry about that. Gian's been crazier than usual this week. I think he suspects something and he's pissed off he can't come right out and accuse me of anything unless he catches me in the act."

We had to be careful every time we met up, which meant both of us would take multiple forms of transportation, go in the front door and out the rear or side door of retail establishments, and generally waste an hour or so going somewhere that took twenty minutes. Without question, seeing her qualified as a huge pain in the ass, but she was worth it, one hundred times over.

Tonight she had a friend open up the kitchen of her family's restaurant so she could cook me dinner. I hesitated to go along with her plan until she assured me the owner didn't have any connection to her family. She'd met the owner's daughter in design school, and they closed the restaurant every Monday so it worked out.

I pulled her into my arms and planted a kiss on her ruby red lips. She tasted like wine. "What'd you tell your family this time?"

"That I was cooking for my friend at her family's restaurant."

"Don't you think he'll see through your story?"

"Nope." She waved the spatula at me. "That's the best part. Bethany picked me up, and I did actually cook for her. She's been begging me to give her my family's meatball recipe. I told her I'd clean up and lock the door when I left."

"You're sneaky. I need to remember that."

"Not sneaky. Inventive. Now sit." She swept her arm toward a wood plank bistro table with two folding chairs. Two place settings decorated the table, complete with flickering white candles. "I know it's not fancy, but I didn't want to open up the dining room, and I found this table by the back door. I think the employees sit at it to take smoke breaks."

"You didn't have to go to all this trouble, Carmela. I would've been happy with a sandwich."

I'd take Carmela anyway I could get her these days, which scared the shit out of me. I promised myself after the Laney debacle I wouldn't get sucked into a relationship that had the potential to turn my life inside out again.

For the first time in over three years, I'd stopped checking out other women in bars or on the street. Last night, I purged my phone of random hookups in my life. I liked seeing Carmela and talking to her. She was easy to be around, unlike Laney. I had to walk on eggshells to avoid any topic that would send her into an inconsolable rage.

"That's good because we're having meatball subs." She pulled two foil covered plates from a warming drawer and placed them on the table. "I know I promised some elaborate dinner, but Bethany kept asking question after question so I didn't have time to prepare everything. But I promise you, when our lives aren't so crazy, I will go all out and show off my skills."

Silence wrapped around us like a sheet of ice, freezing our lighthearted conversation in its tracks. I should have changed the subject, but my mind was stuck on repeat. Her words had gutted me from the inside out. There never would be a time when our relationship would be more than forbidden, stolen moments. I could never take her out on a date or a weekend getaway. This right here was as good as it would ever get.

"Yeah, of course."

She grabbed the open bottle of wine from the counter, filled our glasses, and settled into the seat across from me. She twisted the stem of her wine glass between her thumb and index finger, the welcoming expression on her face absent.

"Is everything okay?" I asked.

"What are we doing here, Kon?"

"What do you mean?" I asked, knowing damn well what she meant.

"Us. What is this? I mean, at first, we were working together to get your dad what he wanted so we didn't have to fulfill that stupid bargain we made. Now we're meeting in secret. We're hiding this from my family, from Nico. That was kind of the point of spending time together in the first place. They would find out about us, and your dad could do whatever he does."

Carmela hopped out of her seat. "God, Kon, don't answer that question. Holy shit, I admitted I put together some trap to screw over my family." She started pacing. "I'm a traitor. My family is going to disown me. I can't believe I didn't put the pieces together before. I was so focused on finding a way for Gian to be happy that I didn't realize the magnitude of what I was doing."

"Carmela—"

"No. You don't get it. I'm going to be ostracized. It happened to Nico's sister. She got pregnant and the father disappeared. Everyone pretends like she doesn't exist, and me, well, I did something so much worse. I'll probably be sent to—"

I yanked her into my lap, framed her face with my hands, and she leaned into me, her amber eyes locked on mine. No words could communicate what I felt right then, so I allowed my hands and lips to do it for me.

"I'm not going to abandon you," I whispered, unbuttoning her chef's jacket and sliding it off her shoulders. "No matter what happens with your family, you won't be alone."

"I'm going to hold you to that," she said, her fingers diving into my hair, her mouth opened against mine. Desperation and desire bled together, lacing our kiss with unspoken promises that should never be made given our circumstances, but it didn't stop either of us from making them.

***

"Let me ride in the cab with you."

Carmela shook her head as she locked the back door to the restaurant. "No, it's too risky. Gian will probably have someone check the interior of the cab when I get out. I'll text you the minute I get home."

I spun her around and kissed her for the hundredth time tonight, my hands sliding up and down her sides. I couldn't get enough of her, and every moment spent without her out of my reach, my gut ached. I wanted to glue her to my side, protect her from everything and everyone, and never let her go. Jesus Christ, I was one dumb fucker. This whole relationship had disaster written all over it.

My dad thought my involvement with Carmela would give us access to the Trassato territories, and in the beginning, I thought he might be right. Now I was starting to think pushing Dominick Trassato would end badly for both Carmela and me. I should cut my losses and run away from this whole thing. Too bad I was a selfish bastard.

"You're probably right," I conceded, ending the kiss.

Threading my fingers with hers, I guided her to a street where she would have a better chance of flagging down a cab. A few cars zipped down the road and a neon sign of a diner flickered, but for the most part, the residential street in Park Slope was abandoned.

"You better get out of here." She slipped her hand from mine. "My brother has spies everywhere."

She stepped into the street to look for a cab. The minute her foot hit the cracked asphalt, a black sedan with tinted windows pulled away from the curb, its tires squealing, eating up the street like a beast of prey, filling the air with the smell of burnt rubber. Carmela swiveled in the direction of the sound, and she froze with her eyes wide.

My heart nearly jumped outside of my chest, panic boomeranging through me. I lurched forward, snagging her waist, and yanked her back like a rag doll. Her arms flailed in a windmill-like circle, her scream ringing in my ears. Her body collided with mine, and the oxygen exploded out of my lungs. I cradled her in my arms, her body shaking, the vein on the side of her neck pulsing, and her chest heaving like she had run a marathon.

The car picked up speed, rocketing around the corner and clipping the raised curb with a loud *clonk*. I caught the first few letters of the license plate, AR, before it blurred in the distance, disappearing into the night.

"Oh my God. Oh my God," she mumbled into my neck. She sucked in a breath as if she were trying to compose herself. "I thought I was going die."

My hand running up and down her back, I said, "You're okay. I've got you."

"What the hell was that?"

"Not sure, but I'm driving you home. I don't give a shit what your family or your brother says. Don't even think of fighting me on this, *solnyshka*."

She blew out a breath, her brows bunching together. "Why do you call me that?"

"Because you like it," I answered rather than telling her the truth. The truth revealed too much.

CHAPTER TWENTY

Carmela

"I'm sorry I'm late. Traffic was terrible. I got out and walked the last block. Between all the tourists and the heat, summer in New York sucks." Ava kissed both of my cheeks, her heavy floral scent curling up my nose, overpowering the freshly baked bread smell in the restaurant. "Look at me. My clothes are damp from the humidity."

"You look beautiful, and don't worry about being late. I only got here five minutes ago."

"Oh, thank God." She plopped into her chair, her elbows propped on the edge of the white tablecloth. "I felt like such a jerk making you sit here when you probably have a million and one things to do. I bet you're chomping at the bit to put all those wedding plans you made with Rocco to use."

"What do you mean?"

"You know." She meticulously unfolded her napkin and placed it in her lap. "Now that you and Nico are getting married. I heard it wasn't going to be a long engagement."

"Who told you about that?"

"Oh, was it a secret?" While her voice dripped with sugar, her eyes were like diamonds, hard and unforgiving.

The fact that my arrangement with Nico wasn't a secret didn't stop me from holding out hope I could get out of it. I'd dropped by Nico's house this morning to get his signature on a furniture order, and he acted like a complete and total jerkoff.

He snapped at me about the cost of the sofa and grilled me about whether I was up charging him. He shamed me for wearing a dress he considered too low cut. He told me he didn't like my makeup. Then he had the nerve to corner me and try to shove his tongue down my throat before I left. I shuddered, remembering the way he exploded when I pushed him away.

"Not really. Things aren't final, so I'd appreciate it if you kept it to yourself for the time being."

Two weeks had passed since the first time I'd spent the night with Kon. I had promised Gian I'd give Kon up and stay away from him, only I couldn't. Every day we found ways to be together. A hotel here, another stolen moment in my room, a planned meeting in the bathroom of a club or a restaurant, even a dressing room in the department store.

We were playing with fire. We both knew it, and yet it didn't stop us. I couldn't get enough of him. Every second spent out of his company felt like torture. I counted down the seconds until our next rendezvous, and the minute I left his side, I started planning our next encounter. It was sick. He was my addiction, and I was pretty sure I'd never stop wanting him.

Ava tilted her head to the side. "That's not what I heard."

"What'd you hear?"

"My mom was going on and on about your mom's plans for the engagement party this morning when I called her. You know how sisters are."

"Right."

Evidently, my mom had ignored my request to limit the engagement party guest list to immediate family members and Dominick. I shouldn't have expected anything else. I hated that my family couldn't be like most families and stay the hell out of my love life. I wanted to make my own choices, and I resented not being able to.

I'd always thought I was lucky I loved Rocco, and he was the person my family wanted me to marry. Both of our families had pushed us together from the moment we could walk. Now I wondered if I loved Rocco partly due to the fact that my family approved of him and deep down I was a pleaser. As traitorous as it sounded, none of the time I spent with him felt half as significant as the fleeting moments with Kon. As quickly as the thought flooded my brain, I buried it into a box never to be opened. It felt like a betrayal of Rocco.

Ava flipped open her menu. "I don't understand your attitude toward Nico. I mean, I know you loved Rocco, but it's time to move on, don't you think?"

"Mind your own business, Ava."

Her eyebrows arched and she straightened shoulders, shooting me a cold stare down the length of her tapered nose. "Nico deserves someone loyal who isn't caught up on another man."

I tossed my napkin onto my plate, my hands shaking and my temples throbbing. "What Nico and I deserve is none of your concern."

"Nico won't tolerate you holding a torch for another man."

"Have some class, and keep Rocco out of this. He's dead. He's been dead for three years."

Popping onto my feet, I grabbed my purse from the back of my chair and slung it over my shoulder. Gian hated Ava. I didn't have much to do with her until a little over a year ago, and right now I regretted the decision to overlook all of the things I always hated about her. She was spiteful, she was jealous, she was a bitch, and she'd likely never change. While she was my cousin, I didn't have to spend time with her outside of family events, and I no longer would as of today.

I was about three steps away from her when she said, "Who said I was talking about Rocco?"

I stopped in my tracks and whirled around. "What did you say?"

She folded her arms across her chest, and her plastic boobs shot up her bony chest. "You heard me."

"Are you accusing me of something?" I curled my hands around the edge of the table and bent at the waist until we were eye to eye. "Because the last time I checked, you aren't exactly the pristine angel your parents think you are. I'd be happy to

170

enlighten them, if need be."

Over the last year, I'd learned a lot of damning things about Ava. She laughingly told me about the affairs she had with men underneath her dad, including names and descriptions of what they did. If she screwed with me, I wouldn't hesitate to fight back.

She twisted her bracelet around her wrist, glowering at the wall above my head. "No. I misspoke."

"I thought so." I walked out of the restaurant with my chin high and my five hundred dollar shoes clicking over the floor. Fighting back was empowering. I felt liberated.

When I put a half a block between the restaurant and me, I grabbed my phone from my purse, pausing in the shade of a tree. Everyone thought I was with Ava, which gave me the perfect opportunity to meet up with Kon. There was a hotel right around the corner, which may or may not have been the reason I picked this restaurant.

As I scrolled through my contacts, car tires screeched around the corner. My head shot up, and fear shot through my chest, remembering the near miss the other night. A black SUV reduced its speed, almost coming to a full stop. The dark tinted window rolled down. The silver barrel of a gun peeked out, glinting off the bright sunlight nearly blinding me.

Without thinking too hard, my body knew what I needed to do. I lurched into a frenzy of movement. My phone tumbled from my hand, cartwheeling across the pavement. One stride and my leg jerked, refusing to budge. The heel of my lace up sandals were caught in the metal grate surrounding the tree on the sidewalk.

Shit. Fuck. Shit.

Mid-motion to dislodge my shoe, I heard it.

Pop. Pop. Pop.

A hot, searing pain tore through my upper arm, right below my shoulder. I wrapped my hand around it, and warm liquid seeped through my fingers. Screams echoed through my ears, and I didn't know if they were mine or someone else's. The smell of gunpowder lingered, mixing with the metallic odor of my blood.

Black dots blurred my vision. I gasped for air, but my lungs were tight. I teetered forward. Right before I fell, I stretched out to steady myself on the tree trunk. The palm of my hand skidded down the rough bark, ripping at my skin, and I lost my balance. I freefell, the breeze whispering through the strands of my hair, and I wondered if this was how Rocco felt when Marco DiTonno shot him.

Images flickered through my mind like a movie reel.

Rocco. Gian. My dad's lopsided grin. My mom's golden eyes...and Kon. I wanted Kon with me right now more than anything. More than anyone. He'd help me. I needed him. God, did I need him...

Seconds that felt like hours later, my head collided with the metal grate and everything went black.

CHAPTER TWENTY-ONE

Konstantin

I opened the door, and my entire body sagged with disappointment. I had hoped it was Carmela so I didn't bother putting on a shirt. I hadn't heard from her all day other than a quick text saying she was going to an early dinner with Ava, and she wanted to meet afterward. It was now eleven o'clock at night, and I was coming out of my skin. I didn't want to think about what would happen to her if her family found out she hadn't cut me out of her life.

"Laney, what the hell are you doing here?"

"You've been avoiding my calls. I didn't have any choice."

She twirled her nearly white blonde hair around her finger and jutted her lower lip out into something resembling a pout. I'd seen this practiced look too many times to count, and sadly I used to fall for her shit over and over. Not this time.

I didn't feel anything except relief when I looked at Laney. Relief I didn't still want her. Relief our dysfunctional relationship was truly over. Even before she started doing drugs, her moods were all over the place. One time she destroyed my apartment, slicing sofa cushions, breaking dishes and shattering my shower door because she thought I was flirting with the waitress at dinner.

"Yeah? You could have left me the hell alone."

She pressed her palm to my chest. "Give me ten minutes of your time, Kon, and I'll go if you don't want me here anymore. That's all I'm asking."

I gripped the doorknob harder, eyeing her hand with disgust. "I don't have anything to say to you, Laney. I shut the door on our past years ago, and I'm not interested in rehashing it today or any other day. I've moved on. You should too."

"Please. I need to apologize. It's important to me."

"You have apologized. I don't want or need another apology. The only thing I want is for you to stay out of my life."

"You don't have to be so inflexible all the time." She curled her hand around my shoulder. "What happened to the boy I met when we were younger? You used to be sweet and caring. You loved me."

I shrugged out of her hold. I couldn't stand her touch. "*You* happened to me. We happened to each other, and none of it was good."

"That's not true. We had good times, Kon, really good times. I've forgiven you for your part in what happened to me. I wouldn't have had access to those drugs if it weren't for you and your family. Maybe you can find that same forgiveness for me."

My spine snapped straight. If I had any doubts, that comment told me everything I needed to know. Laney hadn't changed. She still wanted to pin her addiction on me. Apart from the fact that I took her to places where drugs were readily accessible, I never gave her drugs or used them with her. On the contrary, I bent over backward to help her time and time again until I didn't have any choice other than to walk away.

"Laney, I can't go there with you again."

"Why not?" she shrieked, punctuating her words with a kick to the wall. "I'm trying hard to stay sober this time. I'm working my way through my twelve steps, and one of them involves fixing things with you."

The forty-something-year-old woman living across the hall opened her door and peeked out. "Move the conversation inside or I'll call the police. I'm trying to sleep."

I glared at Laney, not bothering to acknowledge my neighbor. "You have five minutes," I conceded in the interest of keeping the cops away from my place. I didn't keep anything incriminating here, but my livelihood and freedom depended on maintaining a low profile and flying beneath law enforcement's radar.

I opened the door wider, then retreated to the living room, leaning my hip into the side of the couch. "Go ahead. I'm waiting. You've got four minutes and thirty seconds left."

Scowling, she took in my blank walls. "You took

down all of my photos."

Before Laney slipped into the world of drugs, she'd spent the majority of her days photographing abandoned buildings. She had a good following and was well on the way to making a name for herself. When she moved into my place, I framed all of her favorites and hung them on my walls to show her how proud I was of her. They became collateral damage the day I let her back into my home to help her get sober nearly two years ago and she robbed me blind.

I ripped all except one from my wall and tossed them in the dumpster, taking pleasure in the sound of the glass shattering and the wood frames snapping. The last one broke the first time Carmela came to my house, and it was kind of poetic, in my opinion.

"I did."

She swallowed hard and smoothed her hair away from her face, highlighting the fine wrinkles around her eyes from years of substance abuse and hard living. "Oh, yeah, I get it. You probably didn't want a reminder of us after things fell apart."

"You mean after you started having sex with random people in exchange for drugs while we were still together."

"It was only one person, and it only happened once. He's not part of Lucas' life in case you're wondering, and that's the way I want it."

"I thought you said you didn't know who the father was." I shook my head, disgusted with her and myself. "Jesus, so many lies, Laney. How do you keep track?"

"I know. I know. I lied about that and a lot of other things. I guess that's part of the reason I'm here today. I wanted to come clean and see if you'd give me another chance."

I pushed away from the sofa, standing with my feet wide apart and my hands curled into fists. She needed to get the fuck out of my face. I couldn't stand looking at her. What I felt for her had died a long-drawn-out death. "You've got to be kidding me. You can't seriously believe I'd consider going anywhere near you again."

Laney crossed the room and grabbed my hands. "I did a lot of shitty things when I was high, but that person, that girl, wasn't me. I love you. I've always loved you. I got lost somewhere along the way. I need to make it up to you. I'll do anything to prove I'm a better person, worthy of your love." She cleared her throat. "Did you know I named my son after you? Lucas Konstantin. I wanted him to be yours so damn bad."

I yanked my hands from hers. I definitely didn't want to talk about her son.

"Laney, it's too late for this. I can never go back. Any love I had for you is gone, and even if it weren't, I'm with someone else now. She's important to me."

"I know. I heard, and God, Kon, it kills me to think about you loving someone else."

"How the hell did *you* hear about it?"

"I overheard your dad talking about it with my mom. That's why I'm here. I wanted to get my life in order and have a year of sobriety under my belt before I approached you. When your dad inferred that you were serious about this woman, I knew I needed to do something before I lost you forever."

I rubbed my temples. Being around Laney was like being near a black hole. She sucked all of my energy. "You've already lost me. Nothing you say or do will change that. You need to leave."

Huge tears splashed down her face. "Wait. Please. Don't do this to us. I need you in my life. I've spent the last month replaying everything that happened and losing you killed me. It still kills me to think that I threw us away chasing my next fix. That part of my life is over. I promise you. I won't go back there again. I have too much to lose."

A tentative knock sounded at my door.

Dammit.

The last thing I needed was Carmela to show up right now and get the wrong idea about Laney being here. We had enough shit stacked against us without adding misunderstandings into the mix.

"Don't answer that. We're not done talking," Laney ground out when I didn't make any move toward the door.

Remorse and ruin were eating at my insides like a festering wound. "Jesus, Laney. I can't rehash this bullshit with you again."

Bang. Bang. Bang. "Open the fucking door, Kon. I hear you in there. We need to talk. It's important."

"It's my sister. You need to go," I muttered, crossing the room and opening the door.

"Kon," Evie said, her eyes ping-ponging between Laney and me. Her hair was disheveled, and mascara ringed her eyes. "Who's she?"

"No one. *She* was leaving." I glared at Laney and

pointed at the still open door.

Laney rubbed her hands over her tear-stained face and headed to the door. "Can we continue this conversation later?"

"Just go, Laney."

"I'll go, Kon, but this isn't over." She paused with one hand on the door handle. "I'm not giving up on us. I made that mistake once. I won't do it again."

I flexed my hands, checking my desire to throw her out the fucking door. Like always, Laney had piss poor timing. I didn't want Evie hearing any of this shit. Inevitably, it would trickle back to Carmela, and that would only complicate our relationship further.

Worst of all, Laney was a loose cannon. I used to blame some of her crazier behavior on her being artsy and feeling her emotions so deeply. Now I was older, and I knew better. She wasn't right in her head.

"Don't meddle in my life, Laney. I mean it. I won't be nice this time. Things will be ugly."

"We'll see."

The second she stepped over the threshold, I slammed the door closed. The look on Evie's face told me everything I needed to know. She was fucking pissed, which could only mean Gian had found out about Carmela and me. I paused near the door, buying time before diving into another confrontation. At least she came rather than Gian, because a confrontation between the two of us would end with guns drawn.

"Who was she?"

"Nobody important."

"Are you seeing that woman?"

"Why the fuck do you care, Evie? Just get to the point of your visit. I'm tired and I've had a shit night."

"Don't be an ass, Kon. I'm not here for your benefit or mine."

"Then why are you here?" I grabbed a beer from the refrigerator and popped it open. "Because I distinctly remember you telling me I was dead to you."

"Carmela was hurt today, and I thought you'd want to know." She started pacing, rubbing her hands on the thighs of her dark blue jeans. "Maybe I was stupid to come here. Gian will flip if he finds out, and then you had that woman here, so maybe you don't care and I wasted my time."

I grabbed her arm. "Stop rambling and tell me what the hell you're talking about. What do you mean she was hurt?"

"Holy fuck, Kon. I was so scared. She's my best friend." She covered her mouth with a shaking hand.

"Evie. Tell. Me. What. Happened."

"She's in the hospital. When Gian called me, I was freaking out. I thought she was going to die, and we got in that fight last week. I'm such an idiot…"

Evie's voice droned on and on, and I didn't hear a single word. My blood turned to ice. My stomach clenched, my throat constricted, and my chest felt like I couldn't take in enough air.

"Evie," I said, my voice hoarse, "you're not

making any sense. Why is she in the hospital?"

"Oh my God. It was so terrible. She was leaving a restaurant and someone drove by and sprayed a few shots. She was hit, and—"

I yanked on my hair, not caring if I ripped it out of my fucking head. She had inched her way deep under my skin, and I was a fucking goner where Carmela was concerned.

Evie hauled me into a one armed hug. "I'm sorry I'm rambling. You look sick. She's okay. I promise. The bullet grazed her arm. She fainted and hit her head, so she has to stay the night in the hospital. She'll be fine."

I backed into the stool sitting at the edge of the counter. Too many questions banged around in my head, and I didn't know where to start. "Do they know who did it or was it random?"

"They don't know, but Gian has put everyone on this. He'll figure it out." She picked at a loose thread on her jacket. "I need to ask you something and I don't want you to freak out, okay?"

"I already know what you're thinking, so don't bother trying to sugarcoat it. I didn't have anything to do with this and I'm ninety percent sure Dad didn't either."

"Can you ask him?"

"Fuck, Evie. He's a prick, but he doesn't do anything unless it's in his financial interest, and hurting Carmela would guarantee he never did business with the Trassatos."

I disregarded the conversation I had with him when he found out about her pending engagement to Nico. While he might lash out if he didn't get what he wanted, it hadn't come to that yet, and I had no intention of letting her marry Nico. Ever. Thinking about Nico touching her made me want to put a bullet in his head.

"I believe you."

I snorted. "Yeah, right."

"Kon, I know things have been strained between us, and I hate it. Maybe it can change at some point."

I wasn't in the mood for this right now. I needed to see Carmela with my own eyes and make sure she was okay.

"Can I see her or will your husband try to kill me?"

"I was wondering when you'd ask." A gentle smile broke across her face, and she pulled a piece of paper from the pocket of her jacket. "Gian has a guard outside her room, but there's a shift change between midnight and one. Carlo will be on duty and he's lazy. There's a fifty percent chance he'll abandon his post for coffee or the bathroom."

"Great. Now I have to make sure Gian's guys do their job."

She smacked me on the arm. "Be nice. I'm helping you."

"Why exactly are you helping me? I thought you hated me. I thought you didn't trust me around your friend. I'm toxic, remember?"

She shrugged and a rose-colored blush dusted her cheeks. "I guess you probably heard that."

"I'm not admitting to anything."

"Yeah, well the jury is still out on you."

"Fine." I took the folded piece of paper from her

hand. "Is hospital and room number on here?"

"Not so fast." She grabbed it back from me. "First, you have to tell me what was going on with that woman because if you're screwing around with Carmela's emotions or playing games, I'm not letting you anywhere near her. Ever."

"It's none of your business."

"Then you're not getting anything out of me."

"Look, Evie. Carmela's important to me."

"Important enough to stop playing games and tell the truth for once? Because I'll tip Gian off if I think you're dicking her around."

"Jesus Christ." I struck the countertop with the palm of my hand, the stinging sensation vibrating up my arm. "I don't want to talk about Laney. We have a long, sad story, but here's a short and sweet summary. We dated years ago. It ended when I found out she fucked around behind my back and got pregnant. She showed up out of the blue tonight, and I only answered the door because I was hoping it was Carmela. Is that enough information for you? Or do you want me to spill some blood and tears too?"

She blinked. "I'm not trying to be judgmental, Kon."

"Then stop," I snapped.

She slid the paper across the countertop. "I don't believe you're fully invested in your relationship with Carmela. Not entirely anyway, but she begged me to tell you what's going on, and I respect her right to do what she wants with her life even if I think it's a mistake."

"Thanks. That's a backhanded compliment if

I've ever heard one."

"Don't hate me for being skeptical. You did a lot of crappy things, and in spite of them, I still came to your house tonight." She glanced at the floor. "Look, I haven't forgotten the person you were before you got sucked into Dad's world. Maybe he's still in there somewhere. Carmela seems to think so." She tapped her finger on top of the paper. "Everything you need to know is on there."

My muscles unwound and I blew out a choppy breath. "Thanks, Evie. I owe you."

"Don't make me regret this."

I pulled her into a hug and kissed the top of her head. "I won't. I promise."

She stepped out of my hold. "If you get caught—"

"I know, I know. You didn't tell me a thing. I haven't talked to you in over a year. You hate my guts. You'd kill me if you had the chance. I think that about covers it, don't you?"

"Thanks for understanding." She rubbed her hands together. "I want to be clear that my coming here tonight doesn't mean I forgive you or that I approve of whatever you have going on with Carmela."

"Don't worry. You've made all of that crystal clear more than once."

CHAPTER TWENTY-TWO

I sat around the corner from Carmela's room in a small waiting room with a Yankees baseball cap pulled low over my eyes and a magazine in my lap. A man in the corner slept with his head propped against the wall. The steady purr of his snore had started an hour ago.

Midnight had come and gone, and the man guarding Carmela's door hadn't left his post. I suspected he was far more attentive than Evie gave him credit for. The constant chimes of the nurse call button and smell of burnt coffee were the only things keeping me awake.

I'd lost all hope I would be able to sneak into Carmela's room. I should give up on this nonsense and go home. Nothing good would happen if someone from the Trassato family spotted me.

"Hey, man," someone said in a hushed voice right outside the door to the waiting room. "What are you doing here?"

"We have some stuff to discuss."

I leaned forward and caught the profile of Carlo's face.

"I can't talk here. Let's take a walk when my shift ends," Carlo replied. "You know how Gian is about his sister. He's probably paying the hospital staff to call him if I leave my post. He's such a Mustache Pete these days."

"Yeah. He has more to prove now after marrying a *Madigan*."

"Stupid fucking move." Carlo shook his head. "But it doesn't change the fact that he'll beat my ass if I disappear."

"Ten minutes. That's all I need. If Gian calls, tell him you ate some bad food in the cafeteria and had to take a shit."

Sighing, Carlo said, "Let's talk in the bathroom to make it look legit."

"You're such a pussy."

"*Va fa napole.*"

When the shuffle of their leather shoes faded, I tossed the magazine on the end table and took off toward Carmela's room. There was no way I could get in and out of her room in ten minutes, but fuck it. I needed to see her. I'd deal with the fallout later.

I closed the door softly behind me. For a few beats, I stood at the entrance of the room, watching Carmela in her bed. She was on her side, facing away from the door.

Nervous to move further into the room, I rubbed my hands down my thighs. I didn't know what to say to her. Someone shot her. She was probably scared shitless, and I wasn't there to protect her. In all likelihood, I'd never be there. Her family wouldn't accept me, which was a big fucking deal in Carmela's world. She acted tough, she went behind their backs on occasion, but she loved them fiercely. I could see that, and she wouldn't consider marrying Nico if that weren't true.

She rolled onto her back. "Kon, is that you?" Her voice was weak and gravelly.

"Yeah." I walked over and balanced my hip against the plastic railing on the side of her bed, studying her face. A purplish bruise covered the right side of her forehead along with a few scratches, and dark circles stained the fragile skin underneath her eyes.

"I don't get it." Her head moved haltingly from side to side. "Why are you here?"

"I was worried about you."

"How'd you find out I was here?"

"Evie told me what happened and where I could find you. I've been sitting down the hall for over three hours, waiting for an opportunity to slip into your room."

"Sorry about that. Gian's freaking out and acting like his usual overbearing self. He wanted to put two guards outside my room and one by the elevator. Evie had to drag him out of the room earlier, and I didn't really believe she'd get in touch with you."

"I can't blame him." I swallowed, my throat clogging with emotion. If I were in charge, I would have people crawling all over this place protecting Carmela. One fucking person wasn't enough to keep her safe, especially when the jackass didn't need much persuasion to abandon her. A lot could happen in ten minutes. "Does he have any leads on the shooting?"

"No. Not that I heard, and he wouldn't tell me anyway. He treats Evie and I like we're made of glass."

"Did you see the person who shot you?"

"No." She closed her eyes. A shudder rippled through her body and her breathing quickened. "The window rolled down and a gun slid out the window. My shoe got stuck in a metal grate and I-I couldn't move. I was scared out of my mind. Then there was the pain and I was falling. I woke up at the hospital. That's it."

I sat in a chair next to her bed and smoothed her tangled hair away from her face repeatedly, being careful not to put too much pressure on her. "I'm sorry, Carmela."

"It's not your fault. More than likely, it was completely random. I could've been anyone, and I was in the wrong place at the wrong time."

Tears beaded in the corners of her eyes, and I felt like I was coming out of my skin. If I found the person who did this to her, I'd rip him apart piece-by-piece and flush the remains down the toilet like the disgusting piece of shit he was.

"You're probably right. Get some rest. I'll sit here for a while longer."

My gut screamed at the lie. I'd bet my life she was the target. I couldn't speculate about the motivation, though. There were so many possibilities, I didn't know where to start.

I had enemies. Nico had enemies. Her entire

family had enemies. As a rule, the Italian mafia didn't touch wives or sisters. With a few exceptions, the women stayed above the fray, living a more traditional, sheltered life. Gian knew this, which meant he'd be gunning for me. He'd try to lay the blame for this in my lap, and I couldn't prove him wrong.

Renzo DiTonno likely wanted to kill me. His family had demoted him to a lowly soldier. Renzo wasn't my only enemy floating around either. I'd pissed off plenty of people by refusing to do business with them. I could probably fill an entire notebook with names of people who didn't like me.

I lowered the safety railing and rested my head on the mattress. This was fucked up. I'd never forgive myself if my involvement in her life caused this. It was one of the reasons I hadn't jumped into anything vaguely resembling a relationship since Laney. Being part of my life wasn't easy.

I disappeared without explanation from time to time, I traveled a shit ton, and I had more than my fair share of blood on my hands, but that wasn't the worst part. My world opened doors to destructive shit like drugs. Laney was a testament to the hazards of being in my life.

"How long are you staying?" she whispered about twenty minutes later.

I glanced at the rectangular window in the door. Carlo hadn't returned. Anger pulsed through my veins. There was no way I'd leave her unprotected. I'd stay here until Gian or someone else in her family returned, and I'd tell him exactly what I thought of his half-assed attempt at protecting his sister.

"Until morning."

Her eyes widened.

"I'm well aware of what's gonna happen in the morning, and I don't care. I'm not leaving you here alone."

"Do you think I'm in danger?" she inquired, her voice unsteady.

"I don't want you to be alone. Let's leave it at that."

"All right." She scooted away from me and patted the open sliver of bed. "If you're going to stay, share the bed with me."

"You're hurt."

"Please. I need you. I don't want to be alone either."

Unable to resist her pleading tone and the fear in her eyes, I climbed into the bed and wrapped my arm around her. I breathed in her lemon scent now mixed with the smell of antiseptic and my muscles unfurled for the first time since Evie banged on my door and told me someone had shot Carmela.

"Now sleep or I'm leaving."

Within minutes, she was back asleep, her ribcage rising and falling steadily against my body.

"I love you, Kon," she mumbled so softly against my chest I almost missed it.

She loves me.

A sharp pain ricocheted through me and my gut twisted into knots. I froze mid-stroke of my hand on her back, clueless how to respond. Everything inside of me screamed to claim Carmela as my own, damn the consequences.

Without a doubt, I felt something close to love, but I wasn't one hundred percent there, and I refused to toss the words around casually only to take them back when it suited me. Too many people had done that to me, and I wouldn't make the same mistake.

Laney told me she loved me thousands of times. My parents claimed to love me. Even Evie had promised we'd be there for each other. All of them, the people I thought would stick by me and love me forever, turned on me or picked something over me.

Laney loved drugs more than me. My dad loved me for what I could do for his business. My mom loved the money I sent her. Evie loved me until it was inconvenient.

The soft purr of a snore floated through the room, and I realized she didn't expect a response, which only left me wondering what I would have said if she were awake right now.

CHAPTER TWENTY-THREE

"What the *fuck* are you doing here?"

My eyes blinked open, my half-asleep brain trying to catch up with everything. My arm hung limply over Carmela's waist. My mouth felt like cotton, and my back ached like a motherfucker.

I propped up my torso on my elbows, and my gaze collided with Gian's impassioned glare. Before I could scramble to feet, he was already across the room. Evie stood frozen near the door, her dark eyes wide.

Gian's fingers curled around my shirt and he jerked me to my feet. "Are you deaf? I asked you a question."

"Get off of me," I growled, my hand clamped around his wrist.

"Go fuck yourself."

His fist smashed into my jaw. I stumbled and my hip rammed into the side of Carmela's bed.

"Stop it. Stop it. Stop it!" Carmela chanted, her

voice rough from sleep. "Don't fight. Please don't fight. I asked him to come here, Gian. If you're going to be mad at someone, be mad at me."

Gian stalked toward me. "Carmela, this doesn't concern you."

"Like hell it doesn't!" she yelled. "This is *my* life. I get to call the shots, not you."

"No. You don't. Not anymore. You're incapable of making good decisions. You didn't fool me. You've been sneaking around to meet this piece of shit. I can't prove it, but I know it. You're ruining your life for a man who's using you. He knows you're vulnerable. He thinks you're the weak link. He doesn't care about you. He will *never* care about you."

My muscles rattling with anger, I lurched forward and Carmela gripped a chunk of my shirt, trying to hold me back. She didn't need to. I wouldn't fight her brother in the hospital while she looked on. She'd been through enough over the past few years, although that didn't mean I'd let him take another cheap shot at me or spew lies.

I shoved his shoulder. "Back off. You don't know shit."

"This is over. Stop fucking with my family!" he shouted, his chest heaving and his fists up, ready to take another swing.

I tugged on the bottom of my shirt and strolled by him, heading to the door. This wasn't the time or the place to get into this. Carmela didn't need to see this and neither did Evie.

I paused at the threshold and glanced over my shoulder. "You don't own me, Gian. You can boss your little fucking soldiers around all you like, barking out orders and playing out some sick superiority fantasy, but I won't bow down to you or anyone else in your family."

Gian charged forward, his finger pointed me. "You will not look at my family. You will not talk to my family. You will not think about my family. You got that?"

"Gian," Evie said, latching onto his shoulder, "this is not the time or the place."

He shrugged her off. "He's putting my sister in danger. I'm not going to stand around and let it happen."

"Put her in danger?" I stared down my nose at him, then cocked an eyebrow. "No, you have our roles reversed. Your piece of shit guard left her alone for over an hour last night, so don't lecture me on endangering Carmela."

"You're lying."

"Think about it. How else would I have got into this room? You know what's even more pathetic? He didn't even bother to peek in the door before he took off this morning. If this is how your soldiers follow your orders, maybe you need to consider another profession, *capo*," I drew out the word, mocking his title. "But don't take my word for it, ask Carlo about his impromptu bathroom meeting last night, or better yet, pick his brain about what he thinks of you marrying a *Madigan*. While I'm not entirely clear what it means, I'm damn sure it wasn't flattering to *my sister* or you."

I didn't wait for his response. I'd said enough. There was no way I'd heed his demand and stay away from Carmela. As far as I was concerned, she was mine. Sure, I had dicked around for over a year trying to get my head in the right place before I claimed her. I even tried to find a way out of the arrangement she made with my dad, but I was done denying myself. I wanted Carmela, and the Trassatos would have to pry her out of my cold, dead hands before I'd willingly give her up.

I stomped down the hall, adrenaline rushing through me. With each step, my anger and frustration climbed higher and higher. My fingers itched with the sickening urge to put my fist through the wall over and over until my knuckles were bloody and pain replaced the fear that I was going lose Carmela before I had her.

Gian would have his little soldiers crawling up my ass like flies on shit. It would be virtually impossible to get Carmela alone any time in the near future. I wasn't going to roll over and give up. I'd storm her fucking house with a gun and kidnap her if I had to.

"Kon. Kon! Wait up," Evie called after me, her shoes squeaking on the white and green checkered linoleum floor.

"Not now, Evie."

I picked up my pace, not interested in another lecture from Evie today. I got her message loud and clear. She hated me for not telling her the truth about our dad and meddling in her relationship with her ex. I accepted I hurt her, but she refused to allow me to make it up to her, and when push came to shove, she wouldn't stick up for me. In my mind, we could mutually write each other off. I was officially done with her and she was done with me. I was wasting my time trying to get back into her good graces.

"Then when, Kon?" She tugged on the back of my shirt and I swatted her away.

"Never. How's that sound?"

She staggered, her face pale, and her eyes glossy. "Why are you being like this?"

"Being like what, Evie? You don't want me in your life, and I'm respecting your wishes."

"Ugh. I'm the one who should be mad at you. I helped you, and you repaid me by throwing my duplicity in my husband's face this morning. You should have been gone by now."

I bit back all the shit I wanted to say to her. "I don't turn my back on people I care about. Don't you get it? Carmela was left unprotected last night. I couldn't let her stay here alone."

"Dammit, Kon, you need to let her go. This will never work between you two. You're dragging this out for God knows what reason. Let it go. If you ever cared about me, you will walk away."

"What about what I feel? What Carmela feels? Do you care about that? Or is this solely about making you and Gian happy?"

"Oh, right." She rolled her eyes. "Don't make me the bad guy. This is a game for you. Dad didn't get what he wanted out of my relationship with Gian so you're messing around with Carmela to make a point. You don't love her."

"You don't know a damn thing, Evie. Maybe if you pulled your head out of your ass for a second, you'd realize the truth."

"And what's the truth, Kon?"

"I wouldn't have come here last night or spent the last month sneaking around to see her and putting my life on the line if I didn't love her."

I turned my back on her and got out of there before she could rile me any further. I hadn't been able to admit it to Carmela or myself last night, but it was the truth. The inevitability of losing her brought it all into sharp focus.

I loved her golden eyes, her sultry curves, her laugh. I loved the way she looked at me like I was the only person in the world.

I even loved our screwed up love story. I didn't regret a single thing that happened between us except leaving her hospital room without confessing exactly how much I loved her because I wasn't sure I'd get another chance, and I needed my sunshine. My *solnyshka*. She was the only good and pure thing in my life right now. Maybe ever.

CHAPTER TWENTY-FOUR

Carmela

"Carmela, can you come downstairs? You uncle and your brother would like to talk to you."

My face visibly wiped of the rage building in my chest over the past week, I made eye contact with my mom. From the minute the doctor released me from his care at the hospital, I'd been a prisoner in my home. Gian had guards stationed outside of our house and my door. He had confiscated my phone and my computer, and he refused to return them.

"I'm busy. Maybe some other day."

"Busy doing what?"

I picked up the design magazine next me on the bed. "Reading."

Sighing, my mom crossed the room and ripped the magazine from my hand. "Stop this right now. I won't let this rift between my kids continue for one more minute. I can't take it."

"Then tell your *son* to stop treating me like I'm incapable of thinking for myself."

"Oh, sweetie." She settled on the edge of my bed. "He's not. He's worried about you. We all are. You could have been killed, and Gian doesn't have a single lead."

"Lucky me. Does that mean he plans to keep me locked away until he has answers?"

She pushed her hand through my hair, and it reminded me of being a kid again. She used to play with my hair until I fell asleep. I'd do anything to feel safe and loved like that again.

"It's more than that. Gian doesn't trust *that boy* to stay away from you. He's not good for you, and your father, well, he'd roll over in his grave if he knew how you've been carrying on with him. He would never approve of a relationship between the two of you."

"*That boy?*" I glared at her. "He has a name, Mom. It's Konstantin. You know that. Don't pretend he's some distant stranger. He's Evie's brother."

She folded her arms around the waist of her black dress. "Are you going to come down and talk to them or should I send them up here?"

"Whatever. It doesn't matter to me."

"At least come down and say hello to Emilia."

"What? Emilia's here?"

"Yes."

"How'd that happened?"

Emilia was Dominick's daughter. She was five years younger than me, and she had disappeared the night before her nineteenth birthday party.

Dominick pretended as if she didn't exist. His house had been stripped of all her pictures and he'd turned her bedroom into an exercise room.

Until two years ago when I overheard my mom and dad saying she had married some guy in California I had assumed she was dead. We'd never been overly close. She kept to herself, barely interacting with anyone at family events other than Letizia, and she disappeared from our life right after Emilia. My mom claimed Emilia was introverted because she lost her mom when she was thirteen years old. To me, she came off as dark and full of disdain for all of us.

"I'm not sure. Dominick doesn't confide in me."

"Fine. I'll come down, but only because I want to see Emilia." For the first time in my life, I felt a weird kinship with her. My family was suffocating me, and I suspected she might be able to relate.

Before I made it to the great room, Gian pulled me into my father's mostly abandoned study. Inside, Dominick sat behind the desk, his imposing demeanor and dark scowl claiming it as his own. Behind him, Sal and Tony stood on either side of him like centurions, their backs to the wall, one hand tucked inside their jackets, poised to kill any threat to the head of our family.

"Carmela." Dominick's gravelly voice echoed through the room. "Please take a seat."

I glanced back at my brother, and he merely nodded his head. He'd given me the cold shoulder since he discovered Kon in my hospital bed. His betrayal and refusal to support me made my heart ache.

I slid into the chocolate leather chair across from him, and Gian took the seat next to me. I had no illusions this meant he was on my team and intended to support me. Dominick ruled this family with a heavy hand, and whatever I said right now wouldn't alter the outcome.

"I'm disappointed in your refusal to honor your dad's wishes to marry Nico," he started. "We've protected you and gave you unprecedented freedom after Rocco's death. We've let you have your design business you didn't think we knew about. We permitted you to live in the city until your dad died. We gave you a little leeway in your relationship with the Trincher man. However, all of that is over. You're going to do the right thing now."

"What's that?" I asked him, although I already knew the answer. I wanted him to spell it out and make it absolutely clear that he expected me to marry someone I didn't like or want as though we lived in the Victorian era, not the twenty-first century.

He tugged on the cuffs of his white shirt and slid his suit-clad elbows across the glossy desk. "Let me lay it on the line for you. I'm hosting an engagement party for you and Nico in three days. You will marry him by the end of the month in a small ceremony in your backyard. The plans are already in the works. We don't need or want your input. All we need from you is for you to slip on the dress purchased for you, walk down the aisle, and say 'I do.'"

"No. I won't marry Nico."

"It's been decided, and considering your behavior lately, you're lucky marrying Nico is the only consequence."

"Gian." My head whipped to the side, my eyes meeting his. "You said you'd support me. That you wouldn't make me marry Nico. You're supposed to be on my side. You're my brother."

"I'm sorry, Carmela." The skin under his eyes looked bruised. He hadn't shaved in a couple of days. He looked like crap. "You're marrying Nico. There isn't a way out of this. I can't keep you safe anymore. You need to be under someone's protection."

"This is ridiculous. You don't have any evidence that person targeted me, yet you're keeping me under lock and key like a prisoner, and now you want me to marry some guy neither of us likes so I'm *safe*. What about happy? Do you care if I'm happy? Or is this all about assuaging your conscience and ticking off some mental checklist so you can get to your perfect little life while mine continues to burn?"

Gian jerked back as if I slapped him. "You're acting like a child."

"You're acting like a dictator," I shot back.

"That's enough!" Dominick pounded his fist against the desk; the metal penholder rattled then tipped over, scattering pens all over the top. "You need to learn your place, Carmela."

"Where's that?"

"Exactly where we tell you. You'll marry Nico. You'll come to the engagement party in three days. You'll walk down that aisle and say 'I do,' and you'll do all of it with a goddamn smile on your face."

"And if I don't?"

"Konstantin Trincher will pay for your sins against our family."

"What's that supposed to mean?"

Dominick rose out the chair, dusting imaginary lint from his suit jacket, his lifeless eyes drilling into me. I'd seen him like this in the past when I spied on his conversations with my father. A shiver darted down the spine. This man wasn't my uncle. He was the one people whispered about in hushed tones full of fear. He was a living, breathing manifestation of evil.

"Don't play dumb." He stalked around the desk, pausing near my feet. "You know exactly what I mean."

My heart swooped and flapped against my chest. I'd stupidly believed I could get away with making that dumb deal with the Trinchers and walk away unscathed. At the time, I wanted to make Evie and Gian happy. Then I went along with Kon's plan, thinking...I didn't know what the hell I'd been thinking, and I didn't care anymore.

I felt lighter around him, like the weight of all the ugly things in my past had been lifted from my shoulders. I wasn't numb. I cared about my future again, and I no longer wanted to blindly walk off the plank, sacrificing myself for my family.

"I can't marry Nico," I whispered.

"It's done. You will marry him; I gave him my word. You will honor it, or you'll be dead to this family."

"I will be dead either way." My lips quivered. "A little over a year ago, I made a deal with the Trinchers. I agreed to marry Konstantin in exchange for them backing away from Gian and Evie."

Gian's head whipped to face me. "You did *what*?" His voice sliced through the air like a physical blade.

"You heard me."

"That's why you're running off with him without regard for your family or our wishes?" Gian shouted.

"At first, but now…" I swallowed over the desert like dryness coating my mouth. "Now I love him."

"That's fucking ridiculous. Do you hear what you're saying? You don't love him. You have Stockholm Syndrome. He trapped you into this arrangement, and you twisted it up in your head, convincing yourself you love him or some shit like that."

"You're wrong. Either way, it doesn't matter. I can't go back on my word. Alix, his father, will come after me. After the whole family. He'll—"

"He'll do nothing." Dominick hooked his thumbs over his shiny black belt. "He's been trying to muscle his way onto our turf for years to push heroin. That's what he wants. He doesn't give a fuck if you marry his son. So here's what's gonna happen. I'm gonna cut a deal with the fucking Trinchers, and you're gonna be a good girl and marry Nico. This is the best offer you're gonna get."

"I want—"

He pointed his finger at me, his face contorting

with rage. So much rage, my blood iced over in my veins, zapping any of my lingering resistance.

"I don't give a flying fuck what you want. You're lucky I don't kick your ungrateful ass outta our lives. You betrayed the family. You shit on your father's dying wishes. You lied to your mother and your brother. You were disloyal to your future husband. But I'm willing to overlook all of that and let that man you supposedly love live on two conditions."

Unease closed around my chest and I could hardly take in another breath. I gawked at Gian, begging him with my eyes not to abandon me. I didn't see any sympathy on his face, only a deep divot between his brows. He wouldn't help me. I only had myself, and I'd be damned if I let my so-called family hurt the man I loved.

I wanted to scream at Gian. I loved him more than anyone for as long as I could remember. As kids, we could finish each other's sentences. We slept in the same bed until we were six. I tagged along with his friends, and he beat the crap out of anyone who looked at me wrong. When our parents confronted him, he'd always say a slight against me was a slight against him. I guess he didn't believe that anymore.

"What do you want?"

"You'll marry Nico quickly and without protest, and that Russian's name will never cross your lips again. You will never see him again, you will never even think of him again. I expect your unconditional loyalty to the *family* and your husband," Dominick said, his voice deadly calm like he wasn't dealing my heart another deathblow. One I'd never recover from.

"What about loyalty to me, your niece, your blood?" I growled, my throat convulsing with the urge to cry.

Dominick pointed a beefy finger at me. "Loyalty is earned, not given. You haven't earned anything."

Gian grabbed my chin, forcing me to look at him. "Don't be stupid, Carmela. Konstantin Trincher doesn't love you. This is your out. They get what they want, you get your life back, and nobody gets hurt. Don't turn your life upside down chasing a fairytale. There is no happy ending for the two of you."

Pain. Agony. Sorrow. All of it slithered through me like poison, tainting my love for my family. Nothing stung as much as finding out my family, the people I put above everyone and everything, didn't give a shit about what I wanted. I was a commodity to be bought and sold to the person who had the most to offer them. Nothing was ever about me. My life, my feelings, my desires were irrelevant.

"Fine. You win. I'll sacrifice myself, but not for family. For Kon. If you go back on your word and something happens to him, you'll regret it. I promise you."

I jumped out of the chair, tears already blinding my vision. I needed to get away from them. My bare feet slapped over the marbled floor with every step, echoing in my ears. When I came to the stairs, I picked up my speed, taking two steps at a time.

"Carmela," a hand clamped around my wrist, and

I whirled around ready to lash out.

"Emilia?" I said, my voice shaky. I took in the shiny dark pixie cut that framed her delicate features. Her petite body was clad in all black just like when she was teenager. Gian and I always referred to her as the dark fairy when we were younger. The description still suited her.

"You're doing the right thing," she said, her eyes darting down the hall.

"Were you spying on us?" I snapped, my hands curled into fists.

"A little, but I already knew what was gonna happen. I overheard my father talking on the phone last night."

"Great. I'm glad after running away you've decided to rejoin us and toe the family line. Isn't that convenient? Is your daddy going to reward you for this little pep talk?"

Pain rippled across her face. "No. I'm only telling you this because I know how evil my father is. I ran. I made a new life for myself. Got married. I thought I was free until I came home after work to find my husband dead. My father killed him."

The air whooshed out of my lungs and I swayed, feeling lightheaded. "You don't know that."

A brittle smile split her lips. "He promised to kill any man that dared to go against him and marry me, and he delivered on his promise. If you love that man, you will do whatever you need to do to extract him from your life and away from our homicidal family."

I nodded, my entire body numb. Fragmented thoughts raced through my head, none of them

207

making sense. I was living in Hell. Right when I
thought I had my life and my heart back, my family
ripped it out of my chest still beating and bloody.

"I have to tell him. I need to say goodbye. I need
closure."

Emilia grabbed my upper arms, squeezing them.
"I'll help you get your goodbye."

"How?"

"Tomorrow. I'll find you."

"Emilia. What are you telling her?" Sal's voice
echoed down the hall. I didn't know much about
him. He was good-looking in a dark and brooding
way, but a little younger than me. He'd been my
father's soldier, and now he was Gian's, and that's
all I needed to know.

"Are you following me?" Emilia snapped. "Did
you get sick of sniffing my father's ass and you
needed some fresh air?"

Sal's lips curled over his teeth, his usually calm
demeanor evaporating almost instantly. "You're a
bitch. No wonder your husband killed himself. I'd
kill myself too if I were stuck with you."

Emilia gasped and reeled back, her hand pressed
to her stomach. "I can't believe I ever trusted you,
Sal. You're a liar and a phony. You sold me out.
You probably led the campaign to whack my
husband." She marched forward, her shoulder
ramming into Sal. "Asshole. I hate you. I'll always
hate you."

Sal stared at her, his face pale and his hands
flexing and curling into fists over and over like he
wanted to wrap his hands around her neck and drain
the life out of her. I didn't understand what that was

about, and I didn't want to know. I had enough problems of my own. Without exchanging a single word with Sal, I slipped down the hall and retreated to the safety of my bedroom.

CHAPTER TWENTY-FIVE

Someone shook my arms, and I swatted them away. I watched every hour tick by on the clock last night until five in the morning when the bottle of wine I had consumed finally did me in.

As a general rule, I never got drunk. I hated the feeling of being out of control. That all went out the window last night when my thoughts and heart were racing, competing for my attention. The idea of leaving Kon and spending the rest of my life tied to Nico had tormented me. Every time I convinced myself to walk away from my family, Emilia's cautionary tale of standing up to Dominick would reel me back in.

I didn't want to worry about my family lying in wait for the right moment to mow down the man I loved. Even worse, what happened if Kon and I crashed and burned? I would have given up everything for a chance at nothing. Between Rocco and my dad, I had already lost too much.

"Get up. We need to get ready," a woman said.

"What?" I mumbled, my voice sounding like I had swallowed a bowl of pebbles.

"Carmela, open your eyes and get out of bed. It's past noon. The day is almost over. We have things to do."

I unsealed my dry eyelids and blinked a few times. "Emilia? What are you still doing here?"

"I'm here to get you. We're going shopping for your engagement dress."

I flopped onto my back. "I don't care what I wear. I have plenty of stuff in my closet. In fact, I think I'll wear what I wore to my dad's funeral. That'll make a statement."

"Yeah, well, do what you have to, but we're going shopping. There's this cute little boutique on Third. You'll love it. It's a great location."

"Wait." I sat up and swung my legs over the side of the bed, rubbing my eyes. "Did you say Third?"

Kon lived right off Third, and she was right. There was a cute boutique right around the corner.

A grin spread across her face, and I couldn't speak for a second. I couldn't remember a single time I'd seen Emilia look happy. "Yes. Third. It's a hip area with lots of interesting people."

"How'd you know?"

She shook her head. "You're so naïve, Carmela. If you want to live in this world, you need to learn to play with the big boys. You can't tiptoe around with your eyes and ears closed. You need information so you can be one step ahead of them." She tapped the bottom of my chin. "Close your mouth and stop looking at me like I'm a lunatic.

You need to get dressed for this to work."

"For what to work?"

Emilia bent over and whispered in my ear. "We're going to walk into the store, pick up a stack of dresses, then I'll disappear into the dressing room, and you'll slip out the side door wearing something entirely different. You'll head out the door and off to your man's place. I'll cover for you for an hour and not one minute longer. Got it?"

I searched her face for duplicity. I didn't see any. "You'd do that for me?"

She rolled her eyes. "Don't get all emotional on me. I'm doing this for me, not you. I fully intend to stick it to my father every chance I get."

"All right. Well, thanks. I guess."

"An hour should be ample time to tell him goodbye and get your ass back to the store."

My head dropped against my chest, my stomach pirouetting with excitement and an overwhelming sadness. I wanted to see Kon so damn bad, but I hated that this would probably be the last time I'd see him. Maybe forever.

"Stop it." Emilia flicked me in the forehead. "I know what you're thinking, and you need to erase those sentimental, weepy thoughts from your brain. You're doing the right thing. If I could go back in time, I would never have dragged my husband into this crap. It wasn't fair. It was downright selfish." She swallowed, and her lower lip wobbled. "Don't make the same mistake as me."

"You're right. I'm fine. I can do this," I declared, even though I wasn't sure I believed it.

She gave a curt nod of her head and pointed to

the bathroom. "Good. Go."

CHAPTER TWENTY-SIX

Konstantin

"Stop calling me," I growled under my breath, declining the call from an unknown number for the third time.

I switched my phone to vibrate. I needed to focus or I'd never get caught up. Alesio had wrapped up the groundwork for the car export venture in Chicago, and I needed to get my ducks in a row for a shipment to Russia within the next week. I didn't want to hit a snag on our first run.

On top of that, my dad was out of town, which meant his work fell on my shoulders. People were bouncing in and out of my office all week, and I couldn't get anything done, so I decided to work from home today.

While I needed to do something about Carmela, I hadn't figured out my next move. I'd been waiting for a signal from her. Clearly, one wasn't coming anytime soon. My voicemails, texts, and emails went unanswered.

My phone vibrated across the desk in my home office a fifth time. I snatched it up.

"Jesus fucking Christ, what do you want?"

"Kon, it's me."

"Carmela." I popped out of my chair. "Where are you? Are you okay?"

"I can't talk now. Are you home?"

"Yes."

"I'll be there in two minutes."

She disconnected the phone without saying goodbye.

I ran to the front door, flung it open, and paced, my heart nearly exploding out of my chest and my nerve endings sparking in anticipation of seeing Carmela again. I felt like a fifteen-year-old boy waiting for the popular girl to notice me, and I'd never been that boy to begin with.

The elevator pinged, and Carmela rushed out, her cheeks flushed, her hair flying like a flag, and a huge smile on her face. The second she crossed the threshold, I yanked her into my arms and kicked the door shut.

"How are you feeling?"

Her legs latched around my waist. "Later. Right now, I need you to take me to bed. I've missed you, and we have less than an hour."

"We need to talk."

"After," she murmured, kissing my cheeks, my lips, my neck, and everywhere in between.

"You drive a hard bargain."

Her hand slipped between our bodies, molding

over my cock. It hardened with every stroke of her hand. Shit, that felt good. "No, that's your job."

I stalked down the hall, my hands in the wild strands of her dark hair. I crashed my lips down on hers, drinking her in and taking everything she'd give me, pushing for more.

I laid us down on the bed, groaning when my body met hers. "Fuck, Carmela, you feel so good."

Her curves were made for me. Each dip and swell were perfectly sculpted with me in mind. The first time I touched her I did it with the intention of satisfying my need for her and moving on. Only it never worked, and every touch made me crave her more and more.

Rising to my knees, I lifted her dress up and over her head, kissing and caressing every centimeter of exposed skin, loving the bunching of her muscles under the pads of my fingers and the soft puffs of her rapid breaths.

It had been agonizing not being able to see or talk to her for a week. I even got in my car more than once intending to drive to her house and sneak into her room, but reality always talked me off the cliff. Gian and Dominick had the house buttoned up so tight, it would have been a miracle if I made it inside alive.

Fixing my eyes on her face, I looped my thumbs under the waistband of her panties. I slid the lacy scrap of material down the golden skin of her thighs, goose bumps spiraling like water down her legs.

I pressed the heel of my hand between her legs, working it back and forth, getting drunk on every twitch of her muscles and flex of her hips.

"I'm gonna miss this, Kon."

I froze for a beat, agony rippling through me. "What?"

She threaded her fingers into my hair, and yanked my lips to her. "Make me feel good. I need this. I need you. Please."

Yielding to her plea, I buried my unease and guided a finger inside her, teasing her clit with my thumb. Her face contorted into something that I could only describe as unbearable pleasure. Her legs fell to the side. Her body twisted and squirmed, and a moan spilled from her parted lips. Her walls pulsed against my finger accompanied by a wet sucking sound. I tore off my clothes faster than I ever had in my life, the urgency to be inside her gnawing at my gut like a living, breathing animal.

I wedged my hips between her thighs, rolling the tip of my cock along her entrance, teasing her. Teasing myself. Then I slammed into her, rocking in and out. Her hands fell away from my shoulders, curling around the sheets, her hips rolling and her eyes glazed. She looked so damn beautiful with her red cheeks, messy hair, and swollen lips. It made my chest ache.

Her pussy pulsed against me, and I thrust harder, my release burning like the fires of Hell down my spine. Her fingers dug into my ass like she couldn't get enough. The headboard banged against the wall. Jagged breaths tangled with moans and groans. Then her muscles tensed, and she screamed out my name. I couldn't hold on any longer.

I threw my head back, savoring the moment,

pleasure tearing through me. Pushing her hair away from her face, I pressed a soft kiss to her lips, showing without words how much I loved her.

CHAPTER TWENTY-SEVEN

Carmela

Lying on my side, I traced the curve of Kon's face, memorizing the sharp angle of his jaw, the slight bend of his nose, the decadent pout of his lower lip. My body ached with the thought of never being able to touch him, kiss him, or talk to him again.

I wanted to tell him I loved him, only I couldn't. It would only complicate things further and nothing would come of it. I had to marry Nico. I had to protect Kon from my family.

"Kon," I whispered, "I have to tell you something."

Firming his hold on my hip, a smirk pulled at the corners of his lips. His eyes were still shut.

"Dominick moved the engagement party to Friday night."

His eyes blinked open. "This Friday."

219

"Yeah." I nodded, my throat dry and my chest caving in on itself. "The wedding won't be long after. That's what everyone has agreed."

"You're going to go through with it?" He sat up, his legs dangling off the side of the bed, his mouth hard. His flinty eyes harder.

"There's nothing I can do."

"You can refuse to walk down the aisle." He released an exasperated growl. "What happened with Gian? You told me he supports your decision not to marry Nico."

"He changed his mind after what happened. He thinks I need someone to protect me, and Nico can do that."

"Dammit, Carmela. You don't need Nico. I can keep you safe. Don't you trust me? I won't let anyone hurt you again."

I swallowed with difficulty, wishing not for the first time I could choose my destiny. "I know, but my family will never let me be with you."

He cupped my face. "My father won't let this go, and even if he will, I sure as hell won't. You're *mine*, Carmela. This is bullshit and you know it. Why do you think I'd let you marry that fucking prick after everything that's happened between us? I don't get where this is coming from. I mean, last week you told me you wanted to try and make this work between us."

"I did, more than anything, but it's not possible, Kon. We're from two different worlds."

"So were Evie and your brother. They made it work."

"We're not them."

"You're right. We're not. I'm not letting you walk away simply because your family has some fucked up notion about who they think you should marry and how you should live your life." He dragged his tattooed hand across the back of his neck, his blue eyes shadowed and full of anguish. "Did you mean it when you said you loved me?"

I stilled, not knowing what to say. I had convinced myself I dreamed the whole thing. I'd been on so many painkillers, and they had the unfortunate side effect of destroying the filter between my mouth and brain. When I remembered it a few days later, I immediately dismissed it.

"It doesn't matter."

"Of course it fucking matters. We aren't puppets. We don't have to do what our families want. The most important thing is what we want, and I won't walk away from you, Carmela. When I want something, I don't stop until I have it. *Solnyshka*, I want you. I want us. You think you need to be a good girl and do what your family wants, but you don't. I'll keep you safe. I'll make this work. Trust me."

I closed my eyes briefly, the passion in his words affecting me more than I could express. I willed it all away, refusing to be a prisoner of my emotions. I had to keep my mind clear and protect Kon from my family.

"I told Dominick and Gian about the deal I made with you and your dad."

"When?"

"Yesterday. They staged an intervention of sorts last night."

"What happened?"

"It was ugly. They weren't happy at all. Gian wanted to kill us both and Dominick...yeah, well, I think he'd have strangled me if we were alone. The good news is that they are open to negotiating with you and your dad provided you walk away and we end everything between us."

"What do you mean?"

I chewed on the corner of my lower lip and forced a blank expression onto my face, ignoring the determined wobble of my cheeks.

Don't cry.

Don't cry.

Everything will work out.

"I don't know the details. They don't discuss business with me. I'm sure they'll be in touch. Your dad will be happy. Everything worked out the way we planned."

"Wait. Are you serious right now? You damn well know I don't care about the business deal. I care about you. I'll deal with my father. He'll push and fight, but he'll do what I want. I control more than half of his business empire and a lot of those people will only deal with me."

God, it was so tempting to give in and let him fight this battle for us, but my family would never talk to me again, and I couldn't lose them. While they were overbearing, they were all I had. They were the only sure thing.

"What about my family? You can't control them. You don't have any leverage over them."

"Fuck your family. They'll come around, and if they don't, they don't deserve your love."

"No. I can't gamble away my family." He didn't understand what they meant to me. Evie told me her parents never married and their dad was absent most of their lives. My family held tight and never let go unless you crossed them, and then you were dead to them. "Things will never work. You know it, and I know it. We have the chance to end this while we're still on good terms without any hard feelings. We should take it. It's the best we could have hoped for."

I clutched my chest, my words literally shattering my soul into a million pieces. While I hurt when Rocco died, giving up Kon somehow felt worse. Death ripped Rocco from my life and there was absolutely nothing I could do about it. With Kon, though, I was pushing him out of my life, and I would have to live the rest of my days knowing he was out there somewhere, yet forever out of my reach, hating me and resenting every second he wasted on me.

He jumped off the bed and shoved his legs into his jeans, with a hard, low chuckle. "No hard feelings, huh? It sure as fuck doesn't feel that way right now."

"Kon, don't be like that."

He scooped up my dress from the floor and tossed it on the bed. "You need to go."

"Kon—"

He tugged on the ends of his messy blond hair like he was losing his mind. "Go. I can't look at you right now."

"I didn't do anything wrong."

"Nothing wrong? So you think it was okay to

meet up with me for one more fuck before you broke things off between us for good?"

I pulled my dress over my head and came to my feet. "You make it sound like I used you."

"If the shoe fits…"

Cries crawled up my throat and no amount of swallowing reversed their course.

"You're not being fair, Kon. What are you promising me? Do you want us to get married? Or is this a fling that lasts until we're sick of each other?"

"I don't fucking know, Carmela. If you have your way, we'll never know."

"And yet you're pushing me to walk away from my family and everything I've known without any assurances? Without a plan?"

"You need a plan? Don't give up. Figure out a way to buy us more time."

"More time for you to decide if I'm more than a quick fuck while hiding in the shadows, dodging my family?"

He ground his teeth together, his head tipped to the ceiling, refusing to answer.

I jammed my feet into my shoes and headed to the door. "I can't wait around for you to figure this out. My family won't wait. Dominick won't back down."

"What about you? You're doing the same damn thing to me. You're giving me an ultimatum, telling me you plan to marry another man unless I commit right here and right now. What is that about?"

"I don't know. I can't think. I'm so confused, Kon." I gulped hard. "And I'm scared. So fucking scared and confused, I can't think straight. Dominick threatened to kill you, Kon, and I'm freaking out. I want to fight for us. I really do, but I'd die if something happened to you because of me."

He strode across the room and pulled me into his arms in a matter of seconds. "Don't worry about me. I can take care of myself, and I'm not demanding you fight for us. You need to fight for yourself and what you want first."

"You have to see how hard I'm trying."

"You've lost a lot over the last few years. I get it, but I know you're strong enough. I remember the first time I saw you. That woman would stand up for herself. She wouldn't marry a man she didn't love."

"You mean when you came to my parents' house with your dad to talk about Evie?"

"No." His hands framed my face so I couldn't look away. "I saw you at a restaurant with Rocco, and that version of Carmela had fire. You laughed too loud. You smiled too big. I loved it. I couldn't keep my eyes off you, and my ex lost her mind."

"Oh," I whispered, my heart breaking a little. I missed that version of me too. Sure, I caught glimpses of her once in a while, more since being with Kon, but for the most part, she was a stranger to me.

"After Rocco died I saw you every once in a while when I was keeping tabs on Evie. You still had that fire then. It had dimmed a little, but it was still in there somewhere. You put a shit-eating grin on my face for a solid twenty-four hours the time I overheard you sticking up for my sister when her ex berated her. Right then, I knew I wanted you. I wanted to taste that fire. That passion. When my dad came up with that bullshit plan, I agreed to it because without it, I'd never get a chance to touch you or be near you. Your family held you too close."

"Wow." I dipped my head, my heart banging like a pogo stick against my chest. "I don't know what to say. I don't get it. Why'd it take you thirteen months to come after me? And then when you did you acted like you didn't want anything to do with me."

"Fuck, Carmela. What was I supposed to say?"

"The truth."

"I couldn't explain what I felt. I was attracted to you. I had been for a long time, although I had no interest in a relationship. I suck at 'em. The one woman I let in ripped apart my life. By the time I'd had enough, she was addicted to drugs and pregnant." He pressed a finger to my lips when I opened my mouth to respond. "The baby wasn't mine."

"God, Kon. That must've hurt. I'm sorry."

"I'm over it. I'm better without her. I thought I loved her, but looking back, I didn't. She was addicted to drugs, and I was addicted to saving her. It was a toxic, co-dependent disaster. I focused so much of my energy into making her happy, fixing the holes in her life, that I overlooked how miserable I was the entire time."

I turned his words around in my head, analyzing them, dissecting them. Then it hit me. Kon wanted to save me from myself exactly like he wanted to save that girl. I was his new project, and I didn't know if I was redeemable. I only felt like my old self when I was with him. She used him as a crutch to fix her problems. I couldn't do the same thing to him.

I needed to be strong. Fuck being the pathetic woman who was waiting for my life to end and blowing whatever direction the wind sent me. I was a Trassato, and we fought hard for what we wanted. Somehow over the past three years, I'd forgotten who I was. Not anymore.

I believed in myself. I believed in Kon. I believed in us. The enormity of what I felt for this man made me so damn happy. Even supposing we fell apart someday, I wouldn't regret him. Being with him helped me find myself, and that was worth any future heartache. Never loving anyone again was a far worse fate than losing love again. I had this one life, and I intended to make the most of it, which meant taking a chance on Kon.

"You're right."

"I am? About what?"

"I'm fed up with being pushed around. I won't marry Nico."

He eyed me skeptically. "Your engagement party is in two days. We need to do something fast."

"No, *I* need to do something. I need to fight my own battles." I snagged my purse from his dresser and tucked it under my arm. "I'll call you in the morning."

"What are you going to do?"

"I'm not entirely sure, but don't give up on me

yet."

"I'm never giving up on you. Come here. I have something for you." He opened his nightstand drawer and pulled out a light brown box.

"What's that?"

He flipped open the box. "Take a look."

A thick black lace band was tucked into the box. "A garter?"

"Kind of." Kon grinned. "It's a gun holster and a Smith & Wesson M&P Model 340 revolver. You can slide it up your leg and wear it under your dress or you can tuck it into your purse." He popped open the gunmetal gray cylinder. "It's already loaded with five rounds of .357 Magnum and the safety is engaged. Do you know how to shoot?"

"Yeah." I nodded, my throat suddenly dry. "Gian taught me."

Kon's light blue eyes burned into mine, studying me for some unknown reason. "Good. This gun is small and light, which means you'll get a lot of recoil. And unlike other guns with a short barrel, it doesn't have big shot deviations."

"Can I put it on now?" I asked.

He kissed the corner of my mouth. "I didn't plan on letting my *solnyshka* walk around without any way to defend herself."

"Thanks, Kon. I love it." I always carried a can of mace, but I'd been skittish since the whole incident outside the restaurant. This would go a long way toward giving me back some of my self-assurance that I could take care of myself. "By the way, are you ever going to tell me what *solnyshka* means?"

Lips twitching and his blue eyes vibrant with laughter, he said, "Sunshine."

"Huh? I don't get it."

"It's a Russian term of affection. When I first saw you, I noticed your eyes. They're gold like the sun."

"My eyes?" I said dumbly, my stomach fluttering.

"Not only your eyes, but everything. You're like a ball of sunshine, making life a little brighter, and I'm not living without you. Okay? So go fight for yourself, and I'll keep fighting for us."

He tilted my face up, making sure I was looking at him. Then he kissed me. God, I was a sucker for this man.

CHAPTER TWENTY-EIGHT

"This is stupid, Carmela. You're making a huge mistake." Emilia drummed her black fingernails on the vinyl seat of the cab.

"I have to try. If Nico backs off, Dominick can't do anything about it. He's not going to force Nico to marry me."

She snorted. "Nico doesn't care if you hate him or if you're in love with somebody else. For him, it's all about power. Marrying you solidifies his connection to Dominick and his rank in the family. The only thing better would be marrying me, and we both know that'll never happen. I'm soiled goods, and my dad knows I'd slit my wrists before I'd let him marry me off to anyone involved in the *family*."

"You never know. Nico might want a way out of this."

"Careful. Your naïveté is showing."

When the cab stopped next to the curb in front of

Nico's building, I paid the driver and jumped out of the car. Nico hadn't answered any of the texts I sent him from Emilia's phone, but all the lights were on in his apartment, which was a good sign. If he didn't answer, I'd use my key and wait for him. We needed to talk.

"You can go home. You don't have to wait for me," I said when Emilia followed me out of the cab.

"Trust me. Anything is better than sitting in that house with my dad. He doesn't talk to me, and I don't talk to him. We hate each other and neither of us cares enough to pretend otherwise."

I winced at her description. My family had imploded more than a little after my dad died. I yelled at Gian last night for not supporting me. More often than not, I didn't recognize my mom. She used to be a source of strength and resiliency. Lately, she couldn't bow down fast enough to my uncle's demands, completely dismissing what I wanted with my life.

"I'm sorry. That sucks."

She shrugged. "Whatever. I don't care. I'll be down the street in that coffee shop. Come find me when you're done."

"If Gian or my mom call you—"

"Yeah, yeah. I'll tell them you're safely ensconced in your loving fiancé's home and far away from that evil whatever his name is. I know the drill."

"Kon. Konstantin."

"Yeah. Whatever. I think Sal's tracking us today, and I know how to shake him."

"What's the deal with you and Sal?"

She whirled around, her face scrunched up in anger, and the tips of her dainty ears bright red. "He's a two-faced piece of shit who pretended to care about me only to screw me over the second he got the chance."

"Oh." I didn't know what else to say, so I stared at her, waiting for her to offer more of an explanation. She didn't.

"You need to wrap this visit up within a half hour or less. I'm tired and people are going to get suspicious if we're gone much longer." She spun on her heel with her hand raised in a halfhearted wave.

Less than a minute later, I rapped my knuckles against the door of Nico's third floor apartment. One knock and nothing happened. Two knocks and I heard a few hushed voices. "Nico, it's Carmela. Answer the door." I paused for a second. "Please. We need to talk."

The deadbolt clicked, and Nico opened the door without inviting me inside. His dress shirt was unbuttoned and untucked, his suit jacket and tie long since abandoned. I'd never seen Nico like this.

"Hi," I said, my voice crackling with uncertainty.

"What are you doing here?" His voice was slightly slurred.

"Like I said, I want to talk. Can I come in?"

He stepped back, letting me into his home. "Fine. Come in. You can join our little party."

I stepped inside and came to an abrupt halt. Ava sat on the black leather sofa, half-dressed and very intoxicated. His sister Gemma was slumped over in a checkered chair with her legs stretched out in front of her.

"Do you want a drink?" Nico asked, dropping a hand on my shoulder.

"No. I'm good. Thanks. What are they doing here?"

Ava burst out laughing, her breasts jiggling in her bright pink bra. Dark makeup ringed her eyes and her red lipstick was smeared across her cheek. "Exactly what it looks like. Nico was bored so I offered to entertain him since you're always *busy*."

"Nico?" I turned to face, my stomach churning with acid. "You're with her?"

Nico shrugged, swaying a little. "It's not a big deal. Ava knows her place. She realizes I need to marry you. She won't interfere."

"Not a big deal? You're screwing my cousin and you don't think it's a big deal?"

Nico grabbed Ava's shirt off the arm of the sofa and tossed it at her. "Get your clothes on and get outta here. Carmela and I need to talk."

"What about Gemma? She's passed out."

"Wake her up. I'm sure your ride is here by now."

"Fuck you, Nico. Why don't you tell her about us? Tell her how we've been together off and on for years."

"We fuck. So what? We've never been together. You're just another piece of ass!" Nico roared, and Gemma lifted her head, rubbing her hand over her face.

"I hate you Nico DeAngelo. This is over for real this time."

"Good. Perfect timing. I'm getting married in a month anyway."

Ava pulled her shirt over her head, her hands trembling and her face white. "Let's go, Gemma. Your brother's an asshole."

Gemma pushed herself from the chair and whispered, "This whole thing with Carmela is a mistake. She's not good for you. You know she's been sneaking around with—"

"Get the fuck outta here! Both of you."

"Fine." Gemma squared her shoulders. "Be my guest. Fuck up your life."

Gemma and Ava stomped across the room, and the door slammed with a heavy thud.

"I won't marry you," I announced, finally feeling like I had enough leverage to get out of this marriage. My brother would never make me marry Nico after hearing about this.

"We've already had this discussion, Carmela, and we came to an agreement. As far as I'm concerned, everything is settled."

"Not anymore. I won't go through with it. You're sleeping with my cousin, and I-I am in love with someone else."

He lifted and dropped a shoulder, the expression on his face calm and bored, but his eyes glittered with undisguised rage. "I don't care. I don't want or need your love. And this man you claim to love, I'll take care of him."

My spine snapped attention. "Are you threatening to hurt him?"

"By him, I want to clarify, we're both talking about Konstantin Trincher, correct?"

"You know about him?" I questioned, shock bleeding from my voice.

His eyes brightened, making no attempt to hide his amusement. "Of course I do. And while I hate the idea of getting used goods, your uncle has agreed to compensate me, so I'll get over it. Money will keep me entertained much longer than a faithless wife. Besides, I figure I can have my pick of women. Nobody would fault me given your behavior over the last month."

Snickering, he grabbed a manila folder from the end table and tossed it at me. Glossy 8x10 pictures of Kon and me spilled across the floor." "Here's some mementos. You can put them in a photo album and look at them in the years to come and remember the good ol' days."

"You're sick. Why would you say something like that? Is this a joke to you or are you so jaded that you don't care about anyone or anything?"

"Look at me, Carmela," he said. "Look into my eyes. I dare you to find any trace of a man who gives a shit. I do what I have to, and you're merely another step on the stairway to the place I want to be."

Peering into his soulless eyes, my stomach heaved with nausea. "Where's that?"

"At the top. I'm going to lead the Trassato family. I'm going to be Dominick's successor." He cocked his head to the side. "Once Dominick's gone, I won't have much use for you. Think about that. You might want to be on your best behavior from here on out."

"A lot can happen before then. Like me shoving a knife in your neck or poisoning your food. Think about *that,* asshole."

I was unable to listen to him any longer. Dominick would have to put a gun to my head to get me to marry Nico. Any potential to grow to like or respect this man was shot to Hell, and I'd be damned if I tied my life to him, or, God forbid, had kids with him. A shiver darted down my spine at the thought of Nico touching me. I surged toward the door, needing to get away from him.

He sprang into action, grabbing my wrist before I got more than a couple of feet. When I tried to wrench it away, his hand tightened, pulling me firmly against the length of his frame. His face crowded mine, and I could smell wine on his breath.

"Don't fuck with me, Carmela." He pressed me into the kitchen table, one hand curled around my neck and the other twisted in my hair, yanking at the roots and stinging my scalp. "I don't give a shit who your uncle or your brother are. With one call, I can make you disappear. Nobody will ever find you, and the best part is I already have an alibi. It's called the Russians," he hissed, the icy tone of his voice making my knees wobble.

"Don't touch me."

His hand tightened around my neck centimeter by centimeter. There was nothing loving in the strength of his grip and the look on his face. I gasped for air. The edges of my vision blurred. Saliva pooled in my mouth.

Oh shit, this was it. The irony of the situation wasn't lost on me. I'd spent thirteen months fearing the Trinchers and what my life would be like if I were trapped with Kon, but they weren't the real threat. The real threat had been lying in wait for my entire life, hiding among the suit-clad men who hung around Gian and Dominick.

"I'll do whatever I want."

Panic bubbling in the throat, I lifted my knee, hitting him in the balls. He grunted and bent over, cupping himself.

I couldn't move for a beat. Pressure built, preventing me from sucking in a breath. Like a statue, I stood there frozen in some weird time warp, unable to comprehend what I'd done.

Holy shit. Nico is going to kill me.

That thought snapped me into motion. I sprinted to the door, running blindly down the hallway. I stabbed the elevator button three times in quick succession, then gave up and darted to the exit stairwell, my footfalls echoing off the concrete walls. Three flights of stairs later, I stopped in the lobby of his building to catch my breath, my hands resting on the top of my thighs.

"Pull yourself together," I repeated over and over, giving my muscles and brain a pep talk.

Seconds later, I heard the rush of footsteps behind me. Before I could reach the gun strapped to my thigh, someone pulled a dark hood over my head and forced me to the ground, pinning my arms and legs to the floor. Rough fibers scratched at my face and flickers of light peeked through the woven squares of fabric, giving me a fuzzy glimpse of two shadowed figures.

I screamed, squirming and thrashing without much success. The fabric clung tighter and tighter to my face until I couldn't tell whether I was suffocating or having a panic attack, but I did know

I was growing weaker and weaker by the second.

"Wrap the duct tape around her legs and arms!" a man shouted.

"I'm one step ahead of you," a woman replied. The ripping noise of tape pierced through my increasingly hazy thoughts.

"Leave me alone!" I squeaked out, arching my back and swiveling from side to side. "Let me go! Please."

"I can't stand listening to this bitch," the woman taping my arms responded, her voice weirdly hollow.

A solid object knocked against the side of my skull. Blinding white pain exploded inside of my head and then…nothing.

CHAPTER TWENTY-NINE

Konstantin

Bang! Bang! Bang!

"What the fuck?" I rolled onto my side and squinted at the alarm clock, blinking a few times before bringing the glowing blue numbers into focus. It was three in the morning, and I had drifted off to sleep a measly hour earlier.

I tossed and turned, unable to quiet the voices warning me something wasn't right. Even after drinking two glasses of vodka they refused to be silenced. Their cunning voices mocked me for allowing Carmela to face her family and Nico by herself. Something wasn't right.

Bang! Bang! Bang!

"Open the door, Trincher, or I'll kick it in. It's your choice. I'm only giving you thirty seconds to decide!" someone bellowed in the hallway outside my apartment. My neighbor was going to report me to the co-op if this shit continued.

I stuffed my legs into my jeans, pulled a shirt over my head, and trekked down the hall to the front door. I glanced out the peephole.

Dammit.

"Gian, can't this wait until morning? It's the middle of the night if you haven't noticed, and as much as I love middle of the night visits, I can guarantee my neighbors don't feel the same."

"I don't give a damn about your neighbors." He punched the door. "My sister's missing. I have a feeling you know where to find her or that she's in there with you."

An icy, sick dread tilted my stomach. I fucking knew better than to let Carmela take care of this shit alone. If I could kick my own ass right now, I would. I deserved it. I should've faced off with Nico, Dominick, and Gian and stood my ground.

I shoved a gun into the waistband of my jeans and flung open the door. I needed to pick Gian's brain for information and then end this conversation as fast as possible and find Carmela myself. I didn't trust Gian's people. I'd seen their less than stellar work firsthand at the hospital, and I refused to entrust Carmela's life to a bunch of incompetent assholes.

"She's not here."

Gian stood right outside my door with a gun aimed at me, surrounded by two guys and one woman I didn't recognize. His dark hair stuck up and his eyes, so like Carmela's, looked wild and haunted.

"Don't lie to me." He grabbed the petite woman

with short dark hair and large wounded eyes and wrenched her forward. "She stopped by here today, right, Emilia?"

"Don't fucking touch me, Gian. I don't want anything to do with this. I already told you everything I know."

"Well then, you shouldn't have covered for her today," Gian growled. "I can't believe we trusted you. You've always been a back-stabbing bitch." His withering stare cut back to me. "Now, tell me where my sister is, Trincher. You're one of the last people to see her other than Emilia, and I can't believe a word out of her mouth."

"I already told you she's not here. You can check for yourself," I said, gesturing for him to come inside and search my home.

"Stay out here and keep an eye out for anything unusual." He stalked inside, his hand still wrapped around Emilia's wrist, kicking the door shut with his foot. He pointed at a barstool in my kitchen. "Sit here, and keep your mouth shut unless I ask a question."

"Carmela! Carmela!" Gian called, hauling his crazy ass from room to room. Doors banged shut. Chairs clattered to the floor. He could tear my fucking house apart for all I cared. He wouldn't find anything here.

I folded my arms across my chest when he reappeared. "Are you satisfied?"

"Tell me where she is, Trincher. I'm coming outta my fuckin' skin. Evie doesn't think you'd hurt her, but—"

"Are you serious? I *wouldn't* hurt her. Look,

Gian, Carmela stopped by today. We talked and she left. I never saw that chick, whatever her name is. She came alone and she left an hour later. She told me she'd contact me tomorrow. That's all I know."

Gian's shoulders slumped. "What about your father? Carmela told me about the deal she made with you guys. Would he go after her?"

"My father doesn't know shit about any of this. I told him I had it under control, and he hasn't brought up Carmela in weeks."

He hadn't, which under normal circumstances would scare the shit out of me. The quieter my father got on a subject frequently meant he had something in the works. This time he'd been caught up in the new business deals with the DiTonnos. He'd flown to Paris three days ago to meet with his Russian contacts. He wanted to sort out the additional shipment of cars along with some other deals he had in the works.

"Did you see her after she left my house?" I asked Emilia.

"Yeah," Emilia replied. "She went to Nico's house and I had coffee down the street. When she didn't come back, I called Gian. That's all I know. I've told Gian the same thing a hundred and one times, and he insists on dragging me all over town."

"Did anyone talk to Nico?"

"Of course I did. I'm not a fucking imbecile. He didn't know anything. According to him, Carmela stopped by. They fought. She left. He didn't have much to add. He was drunk off his ass."

Nico was a psychopath. I didn't believe a word out of his mouth. If he hurt Carmela, I would slice him into little pieces and hand deliver his rotting corpse to his next of kin.

"And you believe him?"

"You know what? Fuck you. This is a waste of time. Evie thought this was a good idea. I have no idea why I listened to her. You're a selfish prick." He waved to Emilia. "Let's go."

"Wait." I grabbed his shoulder. "Tell me what you know, and I'll do what I can to help."

He studied me, without a doubt weighing whether he could trust me. He scrubbed his hand down his unshaven face. "I don't know how you can help. You were my last lead. Carmela and Evie haven't been that close lately so she didn't have much information, and I don't know many of her friends from school. I went through her cell phone contacts, and no one knew a damn thing."

My throat thickened and I nodded grimly. "Does she have any enemies?"

"Not that I know of." He paced. "Until recently, she mostly kept to herself. Ya know?"

My mind scrambled through my conversations with Carmela only to come up empty. She had a couple of friends she mentioned in passing and the one who let us use the family restaurant. Other than that, she had her family…and her family's enemies.

My head snapped up. "Renzo DiTonno."

"What?

"Renzo DiTonno," I repeated. "You know, Marco's brother."

"What about him?"

"He harassed her at one of my clubs. Got in her face and roughed her up a bit. He was ranting about the Trassatos killing his brother."

"What the Hell? Why didn't she say something? I'm going to kill him. I'm going to kill Alesio. The fucker. They broke our truce. They broke every fucking rule. You don't touch the women. They're off limits."

"Alesio told me he took care of it. He made it sound like Renzo was demoted or kicked out."

"Why would Alesio come to you about my sister? He should've talked to me."

"We do business together. He didn't want me to walk and cut ties."

"You think Renzo's unhinged enough to go after Carmela?"

"After what happened at my club? Yeah, I do. Even more so, if Alesio actually punished Renzo."

I got my jacket and another gun from the front closet, stuffing my feet into my boots. I was going to kill Renzo. You didn't take what was mine, and Carmela was mine. I'd move Heaven and Earth to get her back.

"What are you doing?" Gian asked as he punched his finger against the screen of his phone.

"I'm going to shut that fucker down."

"I'm coming with you."

I grabbed him by this collar. "You can come with me as long as you agree not to breathe a word of this to Nico. I don't trust that asshole."

"Dominick won't like this."

"Dominick can go fuck himself. I don't work for him."

I fired off a text to Anatolyi to meet me a block away from Renzo's house. I didn't know if Renzo would take her there or not, but it was a good starting point. I hoped we weren't already too late.

Gian grinned. "Then let's get going."

CHAPTER THIRTY

Carmela

I sat on a cold, hard concrete floor with my legs and arms bound. Tape covered my mouth, and I could barely breathe. My head throbbing, I took stock of the dimly lit room.

A cast iron pipe spanned the length of the ceiling, then dipped down the wall, disappearing into the floor. Spider webs dangled from wooden floor joists above my head. The concrete was scaling where the floor met the walls, leaving a pile of chalk-like dust. The damp, musty smell of mildew hung in the air.

I eyed the room, surveying it for weak points. While it didn't have any windows, there was a white wooden door with peeling paint on the far side.

I bent forward, rubbing my elbow up my leg to see if I still had the gun Kon gave me. I did. Thank God. If I could free my hands I could escape, or at the very least, surprise the shit out of whoever put me in this dank hole.

I jerked at my wrists. The tape held strong, and nothing happened.

"Fuck!" I screamed beneath the swath of tape, and it sounded more like a muffled grunt than an actual word. I banged my feet against the floor, twisting and kicking, trying to free them. Nothing loosened its grip.

I rested my head against my knees, tears of frustration leaking from the corners of my eyes. Too bad I couldn't wipe them away and hide the evidence of my defeat.

The self-defense course Tony, one of my dad's soldiers and now Gian's soldier, gave me popped into my head. At the time, I didn't take it seriously, and now I regretted it. He'd spent a full hour explaining how to get out of all kinds of restraints.

I closed my eyes, zeroing in on the memory. Duct tape was only made to be strong in one direction, and it tore easily if manipulated the right way. I remembered Tony demonstrating the move.

Coming to my feet, I lifted my hands over my head and jerked my elbows downward. My arms scraped against my ribcage right before my joined wrists collided with my chest. With a ripping noise my hands flew apart and my elbows bounced against the concrete wall. Holy crap, it worked!

I yanked the tape from my mouth and legs, ignoring the stinging sensation. I grabbed the gun from the lace holster around my leg, and settled in to wait. I waited for so long, I was surprised I didn't fall asleep.

Finally, the door burst open, hitting the wall with

a loud *clunk*. Light from the hall sliced through the room. A woman strode inside, her ominous shadow spilling across the floor. I flattened my back to the wall, concealing the gun and my freed hands between my knees.

Her blonde hair was greasy and tangled, her eyes wide and dilated. She passed a knife back and forth between her hands.

My hands shook as I blindly rubbed my hand along the barrel of the gun, the trigger, then released the safety with a soft *click*. I kept my breathing smooth and steady, never taking my eyes off the woman in front of me.

"I see you got out of your restraints. You're not as stupid as I thought." My eyes glued to the woman, I didn't bother answering her. I didn't want to give her any reason to come after me before I was good and ready.

"Who are you?" I quizzed, trying to bring her features into focus.

"One person in a long line of people who wouldn't mind seeing you dead, but first we're gonna have fun torturing you."

"You're crazy," I whispered, my voice barely audible.

"You know what's crazy?" she shrieked angrily. "You thinking you're entitled to whatever and whoever you want without caring about the consequences. You take and take and take." She stabbed the knife to punctuate her words. "And you only care about yourself." She paused for a painful beat, exhaling loudly, then pointed the knife at me. "Get up. It's time to meet my friends."

CHAPTER THIRTY-ONE

Konstantin

Anatolyi stepped out of the shadows, dressed head to toe in black. The darkness disguised the direction of his gaze.

"What's going on now?" I said out loud, fixing my eyes on the white house with black shutters midblock. All the curtains were drawn, blocking my view. The crickets chirping competed with the distant hum of traffic.

Anatolyi's head swung to Gian and two of his guys. "What are they doing here? You didn't tell me we were working with the *guidos*."

One of Gian's men stepped forward, whipping his gun from his waistband. "Watch your fucking mouth."

Gian planted his hand in the middle of the man's chest. "Not now, Sal."

"Did you hear what he said? I'm sick of these

Russian pricks. We don't need them."

Anatolyi pushed forward. "Yeah? Cover your ears and run back to your mama for another meatball, you little pansy."

"Shut the fuck up, both of you." I dragged Anatolyi behind me before we ended up in a street brawl rather than concentrating on finding Carmela. "We don't have time for this. You can meet up later to trade insults. Right now, we have shit to do. Anatolyi, tell us what you know."

"Not much. Renzo has been holed up in his mom's home for the past two weeks and—"

"He lives with his mom?" I interrupted.

"Not normally, but after Alesio cut him off, he moved into her house. She lives in Florida pretty much all year and only comes home for the holidays. Other than a woman visitor, he keeps to himself. Her car's in the driveway tonight."

"What's her name?"

He smirked, sliding his hand down the side of his neck. "Well, ya see, that's exactly why I don't get why you brought them here."

"Spit it out, Anatolyi," I snarled, my patience dwindling with every passing second.

"Gemma DeAngelo." He cocked a brow. "Does her name ring any bells?"

Gian stepped forward. "Gemma DeAngelo? As in Nico's sister?"

Anatolyi snickered. "Ding. Ding. We have a winner."

"Fuck." Gian tugged at his collar. "This is not good."

"What's the deal with Gemma?" I demanded.

Gian snorted. "There's a lot wrong with that chick. For starters, she's the one who started the war between the Trassatos and the DiTonnos."

"Wait, so Renzo was telling the truth?"

"I don't know everything, but apparently, Gemma gave Marco DiTonno an ultimatum to marry her. When he didn't bite, she pulled some bullshit with Rocco, trying to make Marco jealous. She ended up pregnant, and Rocco and Marco both ended up dead."

"Does Carmela know this?"

"Some. I didn't want to go into the details. There wasn't any point."

"Why the fuck not?" I roared. "Your sister spent years pining after a man who cheated on her. Maybe you should've released her from the guilt years ago."

Gian rubbed the back of his neck and stared down the tree-lined street. "I don't know. Initially, I didn't want to dump another bomb on her. As time passed, I decided it was better to bury whatever happened right along with Rocco. He adored my sister, but I think the pressure of the situation got to him. The guys teased him about his inexperience and being pussy whipped. His need for respect got the better of him."

What a weak son of a bitch. I never cheated on Laney. She was my first, and for years, I thought she'd be my last. Her betrayal put me in a dark place. I made up for lost time and opportunities, screwing women like it was my job, not caring who I hurt in the process. I got it in my head that I could fuck away the memory of her because everything about our relationship turned my stomach.

"Is the kid Rocco's?"

Gian shrugged, his eyes glittering with a thinly disguised rage. "Don't know, and it doesn't change a damn thing. Either way, I don't want her anywhere near my sister. She's a vindictive bitch, and if she's teamed up with Renzo, I will end her. I don't care who her brother is."

"Agreed." I didn't like dragging women down in the shit with us, but I wouldn't hold back tonight. Freeing Carmela was my one and only priority. Failing wasn't an option. I didn't care who I had to destroy to make it happen.

"The clock's ticking. We need to get moving," Anatolyi said.

"You guys go in the front, and we'll go around back," I said, finishing loading my guns.

Gian pulled out his gun. "Tony, take your car and go to Nico's house."

"What for?"

"I want to make sure he's on the up and up. You don't have to say anything. Just shoot the shit with him, make sure he doesn't leave, and listen to his phone calls."

"Got it." Tony opened the car door. "What about Emilia?"

"Drop her off at her dad's. I'll let him deal with her."

CHAPTER THIRTY-TWO

Carmela

"Your friends?" I pried my knees apart, wedging the barrel between my legs. Although it wouldn't be a clean shot, it didn't matter. I wanted to get out of here, not kill her.

"Don't worry." Her chapped lips spread across her hollow face and she looked more than a little insane. "You're already acquainted with them."

"Oh yeah?"

"Renzo DiTonno and Gemma DeAngelo. You know them, right?"

"Sure, but I don't know what they have to do with me being here."

"I'll let them explain."

"What about you? Why are you here?"

"Ya know, I can see what he sees in you," she said, cocking her head to the side and her heavy eyelids drooping. "I remember the first time he saw you. We were at a restaurant celebrating moving in together. He couldn't take his eyes off you. He tried to hide his attraction to you, but I knew him too well for that. I made him pay for looking at you." Her voice dropped, almost like a confession, and she inched closer to me. "If you weren't so pretty, I'd bet Kon wouldn't like you so much. He'd want me back."

"Kon?" I choked out, fear spiking in my veins. "What does Kon have to do with this?"

"Didn't he tell you about me?" I shook my head. "Are you sure? I'm Lanelle. He calls me Laney, though. We were supposed to be married by now. He still loves me, and once you're out of the way, everything will go back to the way it should be."

She raised her eyebrows. "And not only for me, but for Gemma and Renzo too."

"I still don't understand what's going on."

"I like to think of it as divine intervention." She tapped the knife against her leg. "But here it goes. I met Gemma in rehab. Gemma dated Renzo's brother. We all hate you."

"Why?"

"Enough talking. Let's go. They're waiting for us."

I could shoot her and hope I found a way out of here or I could follow her and plead for my life. I had seconds to make up my mind, and I chose to fight. I aimed the gun as best I could between my knees and squeezed the trigger.

The recoil knocked me back and I collided with the concrete wall. My teeth clacked together and I nipped the tip of my tongue. Coppery blood filled my mouth. The gunshot merged with her scream, making my ears ring. Laney dropped to her knees, holding her shin. Blood spilled down her leg.

Pain radiating down my spine, I scrambled to my feet and ran, leaping over Laney's prone form and swerving around the corner. A narrow staircase with wooden steps was at the end of the hall. Before I mounted the first step, arms circled my waist, dragging me to the floor from behind. My shoulder bounced against the concrete, and the gun spun out of my hand.

I rolled onto my stomach to get to my feet. The second I raised my hips, a knee jammed into my back and someone stretched my arms out over my head, pinning them to the floor.

"I'm not going to kill you," a man said. If Laney were telling the truth, it was Renzo. "Not yet anyway. I have a little payback in mind first."

My vision danced and tilted until I brought Renzo DiTonno's twisted features into focus. He was leaning over me, his face inches from mine. He smelled like old cigarettes and stale beer.

"Do you know how Gian killed my brother?" he snarled, his lips curled up and spittle spraying my face.

"No," I whispered, my voice strained from holding back the gag.

He grabbed a chunk of my hair with his free hand and yanked my head up like he wanted to rip it from my torso. "He had his goons beat him until he couldn't move. Then they tossed him in his car and lit it on fire with my brother locked inside. It was a slow, painful death, and yours will be too."

255

I spat on his face. "Fuck you. I didn't have anything to do with that. You're just a whiny *finnochino* taking this out on me since you're not man enough to face my brother."

He smacked my forehead against the concrete. White stars burst behind my eyes, and I pinched them closed so I didn't cry. I refused to give him the satisfaction. If I was going to die today, I'd go down with my dignity intact, fighting every step of the way. I was done being a victim, swinging whatever way fate pushed me.

"That's where you're wrong. I see it as an eye for an eye. Gian killed my brother so I'm gonna kill his sister. Poetic justice, don't ya think?"

CHAPTER THIRTY-THREE

Konstantin

We didn't make it halfway up the front sidewalk before a gunshot rang out. I charged, the plan we made forgotten. My gun drawn, I kicked the door open, and splinters of wood showered the tiled entry.

I paused inside the door, listening, analyzing, and searching for clues. The house was filled with floral covered furniture. It smelled of rotten food and cigarettes. Pizza boxes covered the glossy coffee table.

Screams and shouts carried up the staircase from the basement.

"Downstairs!" Gian yelled, rushing past me.

At the top of the steps, I froze in my tracks. Renzo had Carmela pinned against the wall at the bottom of the stairs and another woman who I assumed was Gemma was leaning against the wall with her arms folded. The part that shook me to the core was seeing Laney curled in a ball with blood dripping down her leg, her face contorted in pain.

Anatolyi nudged my back. "Move."

I couldn't. Seeing Laney there was like seeing a ghost.

"Kon," Laney mumbled, her voice trembling and tears streaming down her face. "Thank God you're here. I knew you'd come for me."

Renzo whirled around, forcing Carmela in front of him like a human shield. He had a knife pressed to her throat. Her dark hair was tangled and blood dripped from her hairline to her chin. My breath stalled like someone had hit me in the gut with a two by four.

"Put the safety on your guns and drop 'em on the floor," Renzo barked.

"No way, man. That's not gonna happen!" Anatolyi shouted behind me. "Don't listen to him, Kon. He's high as a fucking kite. All of them are. Look at them. They're bugging out. This won't end well."

"Do it or I'll slit her fucking throat," Renzo growled, flexing the arm holding the knife. Carmela squeezed her eyes closed, a whimper falling from her mouth.

"Do it," I said, without turning around. With one hand raised, I bent at my knees and placed the gun on the step next to my feet, my gaze glued to the sharp point digging into Carmela's long neck. I heard the clank of Gian, Sal, and Anatolyi's guns banging against the wooden treads.

"Now kick them down the stairs."

Four guns somersaulted down the steps, sliding to a stop against the baseboard near Laney. I still had no clue how she ended up here. Had Renzo and Gemma kidnapped her too? I didn't need any more guilt on my head where she was concerned.

"Kon, I need you. Help me," Laney gasped, holding one blood-covered hand out to me.

"Don't listen to her, Kon. She's using again. Look at her," Anatolyi hissed.

Anatolyi was right. Laney's pupils were like saucers and I could barely see her blue irises. Her hair was greasy and her clothes looked as if she'd been wearing them for days. Shit, she'd relapsed…again. Who the hell was taking care of her kid?

"What do you want, Renzo?" I said, zeroing in on him and Carmela. Laney was a lost cause. She had been for years.

A bitter cackle erupted from his lips. "Whaddaya think I want?"

"I don't know, tell me."

"I want my brother back, but that's not gonna happen, is it?"

"I didn't have anything to do with your brother's death and neither did Carmela."

"Her brother did. Gian had him knocked off, and then you fucked me over. Alesio thinks you're more valuable to the *family*, so he took me to the carpet. He broke me like I meant nothing. What a fucking joke. My brother and I busted our asses for people who turned their backs on us, and for what? Money. Do you know what that feels like? Family. Loyalty. Honor. It's all a bunch of bullshit."

"What does that have to do with her or me?" I shook my head. "Alesio is his own man, and so is Gian."

"It has everything to do with her!" he roared, his lips curling over his yellowed teeth and his bloodshot eyes bulging out of his head.

"Your brother killed a made man, Renzo." Gian stepped in front of me, his hands raised in surrender. "You know how things work. He knew how things worked. We roughed him up. He didn't try to fight us. He understood his duty."

"You mean, you beat the shit out of him and set his car on fire."

"Christ, Renzo. Don't be a *cafone*." Gian scrubbed a hand down his face, the vein at his temple jumping. "We didn't have anything to do with the fire. His car was leaking gas and he tossed a cigarette underneath before he got inside, and it exploded. We gave him a pass. Nobody wanted him dead. We were sending him a message. That's it."

"No. No!" Spit flew from his mouth and his face was beet red. "You're lying."

"No. I'm not. Look at the fucking police report. Ask Alesio. Ask anyone. Hell, ask Gemma." Gian pointed a finger at her. "She knows the truth."

"Gemma?" Renzo said, uncertainty leaking from his voice. "What's he saying? Do you know what he's talking about?"

"Don't fucking lie, Gemma. This has to end. You need to stop stirring up shit. Your brother's gonna cut you off again when he hears about this. Then where will you be? Renzo can't help you. He's shacked up with his parents and you don't have a job."

Her face blanched. "There's nothing to tell. I'm leaving."

She took two steps, and Gian flattened her against the wall. "You're not going anywhere. You abducted my sister."

"I didn't have anything to do with this. Laney and Renzo came up with the plan. They did everything. I told them to dump her ass on the street, but no, they wouldn't listen. Ask Ava. She knows the truth. She didn't want anything to do with it, so she took off."

"I don't give a shit how it happened. You could've called Dominick or me, but you didn't." He rammed his fist into the wall. "Now tell Renzo we didn't have anything to do with the car fire."

"Screw you, Gian," she hissed.

"Tell the fucking truth for once in your life or I'll make sure you don't walk out of this basement alive. Think about what that would do to your son. He's already lost one parent. Do you want to make it two?"

She lifted her head, her eyes narrowed, and her whole body shaking. "Fine. I lied. I lied about the damn whole thing. Is that what you wanted to hear?"

"The fuck?" Renzo growled. "How could you? I trusted you. I love your son like he's my own. I took care of you. I've been paying your rent, buying your food."

"I'm not stupid. I know this looks bad, but don't hate me. I need you in my life. Marco's son needs you. Please."

Renzo's hand dropped from Carmela's neck, the knife dangling from his fingers. Carmela took off, bolting toward me and crashing into my chest. I gathered her into my arms and inhaled her lemon scent. For the first time in hours, my muscles unwound. God, I needed this woman. I needed her more than my next breath, and I didn't give a shit what her brother or her uncle thought, I was keeping her.

"Why, Gemma?" Renzo said sounding utterly lost. "Why would you do that to me? I tore apart my life over a fucking lie."

"I don't know. I can't explain it."

"Your lies ruined my life. I think you owe me an explanation," he volleyed back, sliding to the floor with his back against the wall and his knees bent.

She rubbed her eyes. "You were so mad at me for starting that fight between Rocco and Marco, and putting Marco in that position. It eats me up to think I put this all in motion by hooking up with Rocco. He was so drunk that night, and he had no fucking clue what he was doing. I took advantage of him. I pulled him out into that alley to bait Marco, and he kept calling me Carmela the whole time. Marco followed me out and my world fell apart. I never meant for that to happen."

A harsh breath exploded from Carmela's body, and I tightened my arms around her.

"That doesn't explain why you lied!" Renzo shouted, waving his arms like he was losing his mind.

"I didn't have any choice. Everybody abandoned me when I needed them the most. I was fucking pregnant. My brother had disowned me. Marco hadn't talked to me since the night he shot Rocco. He was dead a few days later. I didn't have a dollar to my name, and there you were grieving over Marco exactly like me. If I couldn't have Marco in my life, I needed you, so I blamed the Trassatos and convinced you everyone was covering up the truth. You welcomed us into your life and focused all your anger on them, not me. My son and I were safe."

"What does this have to do with Carmela?" Gian roared.

Gemma licked her lips. "When I found out my brother wanted to marry Carmela, I lost it. She reminded me of what I did and what I could never have. Rocco and I had a history, but once I realized I could never shake the Trassatos' hold on him, I moved on, and Renzo was there to catch me. But God, I hated her. I still do, and unlike my brother, Renzo stood by me and hated her and her family right along with me."

Carmela's sobs escalated with every confession until her body shook uncontrollably. I pulled her closer, pressing kisses to the top of her head.

"Get Carmela out of here, Kon," Gian barked, snapping his fingers in my direction. "She doesn't need to hear any of this. I'll take it from here."

I looped my hands under Carmela's legs and cradled her body against mine. "Come on, *solnyshka,* I'm gonna take you home. You're safe now."

"Kon, I was so scared. When he had that knife pressed to my neck, I thought I was going to die, and all I could think about was how much I wanted to live for you. For us," she whispered.

"I was never going to let you die. I love you too much to let that happen."

The second the words left my mouth, I heard the soft tick of a gun safety being released, and my gaze followed the sound.

Laney stood across from us with a sneer on her face, her body swaying. She raised a gun, aiming it at us. Time stood still as I gawked at the woman I thought I had loved for years. I felt nothing for her except unadulterated hatred and pity. She was like a cancer that kept coming back no matter what I threw at her, and no matter how many times I pushed her away.

I snapped out of my haze and dove to the floor with Carmela still in my arms. I rolled to my side, absorbing the impact with my shoulder. A gunshot exploded over my head, and white plaster dust showered our heads.

Still shielding Carmela with my body, I reached for the second gun tucked away in the waistband of my jeans.

"Wait!" Anatolyi screamed. "Don't kill—"

With one flex of my trigger finger, I shot Laney. Her body flew back, crumpling to the floor, blood seeping out of her chest, coloring her white shirt red.

Relief flowed through me, the weight of our ugly history finally gone. Maybe I should have felt sadness for her son, but I knew deep down in my soul he'd be better off without her. Laney was a lost cause, and she'd tear apart her son and ruin his life like she attempted to do with Carmela and me.

"You killed her! She's dead! Oh my God!" Gemma screamed over and over. She collapsed to her knees and crawled toward Laney's body.

"Kon, go. Get Carmela outta here. Take her back to your house. I'll call you in the morning."

"Are you sure?"

"Yeah, man." He patted me on the shoulder. "I trust you to take care of my sister. I'll clean up this mess. Sal, call Tony and tell him to get Nico's ass over here and do something with his sister."

Gian kept shouting out orders to restrain Renzo and Gemma. I didn't care about any of that. I had Carmela. She was all I needed. I scooped up the woman I loved and carried her away from this nightmare.

EPILOGUE

Carmela

"Do you think they're going to freak out?" I questioned Kon, drumming my left hand on the table, my shiny wedding ring shooting rainbows over the white tablecloth. Kon had chosen the perfect ring, but that wasn't why I loved it. I loved what it meant more.

Kon swung his arm over the back of the booth. "Do you care?"

I dragged my gaze up to meet his stare. The corners of his blue eyes crinkled and a lopsided smile showed off his white teeth. My stomach flipped over and my heart did this double beat thing.

"No. I couldn't stand the thought of planning another wedding. I wanted to skip to the good part."

He leaned his forehead against mine. "What's that?"

"The part where we start our life together."

He brushed his lips over mine.

"I like the sound of that."

Two months after the nightmare at Renzo DiTonno's house, Konstantin had proposed to me. There was no mention of our earlier arrangement, what our families wanted, or any future business dealings. Only one simple proposal at our favorite coffee shop, one beautiful ring, and a merger of our lives at the courthouse shortly thereafter.

I spent a full year making preparations for my wedding to Rocco and months trying to stop my family from plotting my marriage to Nico. When Kon proposed, I knew I didn't want any of the fuss that went into planning little details no one would remember a week later. I wanted a life with Kon, and I wanted to make it happen before anyone or anything got in the way. I was being superstitious, and I didn't care. I wouldn't give fate a chance to get in my way again.

Alix Trincher hadn't breathed a word about business deals in months, and I had a sneaking suspicion Kon had put a stop to it. The few times I bumped into my now father-in-law in passing, he kept it cordial and polite, and given his history, I was okay with our less than loving relationship. In fact, I preferred it that way. He still scared me.

While my family hadn't professed their undying love for Kon or openly supported our relationship, they stopped putting up roadblocks after that terrible night, and that was enough for me. I had no doubt any remaining reservations would crumble in no time at all, or in twenty-nine and a half weeks to be exact, when our babies made an appearance.

I was pregnant with twins, and I was over the moon with happiness. I wouldn't share that with my family tonight, though. There were only so many surprises they could handle at a time.

Dominick told me in his roundabout way he didn't expect me or want me to marry Nico. Less than a week after the incident, Nico and Gemma disappeared. I had no clue what happened to them, and I didn't care as long as he and his sister stayed far away from me and the people I loved. Even better, Gian stepped into Nico's role as the underboss, and from the little I heard things were going well.

Kon was messed up for a while after Laney's death. He kept second-guessing his decision to shoot her. I understood his anguish. He loved her at some point, and taking her life, regardless of the crap she'd pulled, had to hurt. The father of Laney's child stepped forward, and that was a huge shit-storm. I didn't know if Kon would ever forgive Anatolyi, but Anatolyi was living in his own personal nightmare as a single father, so I think he got his due.

"They're here," Kon said, threading his fingers with mine and placing our joined hands over my lower belly. "Are you ready to tell your family?"

"I think it's too late to back out now."

"You're damn right it is," he growled, nipping my ear. "I'm never letting you go now that we made it official."

Gian, Evie, and my mom waded through the crowded restaurant, drawing all eyes to them. I couldn't blame people for rubbernecking like it was their job. They made quite the couple between Evie's rising celebrity status and my brother's dark, mysterious background.

Gian slid in the booth after my mom and Evie. "Nice restaurant, Kon. I hope you're planning to pick up the tab."

"Considering this is our wedding reception, I don't have any problems with that. Do you, Carmela?"

I elbowed him under the table. "Kon! That's not how we agreed to tell them."

My mom's mouth dropped open, Gian burst out laughing, and a huge smile lit Evie's face.

"You owe me a hundred bucks." Gian nudged Evie and held out his hand.

"You cheated. I know you did," Evie said, rummaging around in her purse, then slapping a wad of cash on the table.

"Stop it with the secrets, you two. Tell me what's going on," I said.

"Just a little bet about who knew their sibling better," Gian said, a smug look on his face. "I told Evie you two would either elope or get married at the courthouse without telling anyone. She thought you would go all out so Carmela would finally get the wedding of her dreams. I was right. She was wrong."

"Whatever." Evie shrugged. "Even a blind dog finds a bone sometimes, and you guys have that freaky twin connection, so I was at a disadvantage."

"Why didn't you want me there, Carmela?" my mom implored, her voice soft, almost fragile. "Are you still mad at me?"

"Ma, I didn't mean to hurt anyone's feelings, and no, I'm not mad at you. We got caught up in the moment, and it felt right," I replied, my stomach stewing with nervousness.

"Baby girl." She slid her arm across the table and grabbed my hand. "You didn't hurt me. I see how much you love each other, and there is nothing I want more than for you to be loved, cherished, and happy. I'm so proud of you. You never gave up. You've had your dreams snatched away so many times, and you kept going. You kept fighting for what you wanted even when we thought we knew better."

"Then you approve of us? Of Kon?"

"Carmela, I love you, and I love Kon even though I don't know him very well because he makes you so happy. Happier than I've ever seen you."

"He does. More than you know."

Kon slipped his arm around my waist and pulled me against him. "I love you, *solnyshka*."

"I love you too."

I meant it. I never thought I'd love anyone like I loved Rocco, and in some ways I was right. I'd always hold my memories of Rocco next to my heart. While he played an important part in shaping my life, I stopped whitewashing all the cracks in our relationship. I forgave him for being unfaithful and myself for the harsh last words we shared, and with forgiveness I found peace and love.

My love for Kon was different, and in a lot of ways, bigger and stronger. We were older and knew what we wanted out of life. We didn't keep secrets from each other, and yes, sometimes his world scared me because in the world of organized crime—Russian, Italian, or any other—there was no security and no guarantees. I learned that firsthand, and I was fine with it. We lived by our rules, and we'd be okay provided we never stopped fighting for each other and our love.

Gian raised his champagne glass. "To the happy couple."

I lifted my glass of sparkling cider and Kon tapped his against mine and whispered in my ear, "To *our* happy family."

ACKNOWLEDGMENTS

Thanks much for picking up this book. I had so much fun writing it and weaving all my crazy ideas together with the help of some really great people:

Amy Bustard for reading this book and brainstorming with me.

Chris for helping me with dialogue.

Felicia A. Sullivan for editing this book and giving me valuable, honest opinions.

All of my relatives. I hope you aren't offended I continue to steal names from our family tree.

Limitless Publishing for being so accommodating.

And of course, to all the readers, bloggers, and reviewers who took the time to read this book. Your support and feedback make all the time staring at my computer screen worthwhile! Next up, Emilia's story.

ABOUT THE AUTHOR

After spending years practicing law and running a real estate development company with her husband, Lisa decided to pursue her dream of becoming a writer and she must confess that inventing characters is so much more fun than writing contracts and legal briefs. A native of Colorado, she lives with her husband and three children in Denver. When she isn't managing the chaos of raising three children and owning her own business, she can be found reading or writing a book or tinkering in her garden.

Facebook:
https://www.facebook.com/lcardiff11

Twitter:
https://twitter.com/lcardiff_author

Website:
http://lisacardiff.com/

Goodreads:
https://www.goodreads.com/author/show/7692079.
Lisa_Cardiff